MOONPENNY ISLAND

TRICIA SPRINGSTUBB

Illustrations by
GILBERT FORD

BALZER + BRAY
An Imprint of HarperCollinsPublishers

Balzer + Bray is an imprint of HarperCollins Publishers.

Moonpenny Island
Text copyright © 2015 by Tricia Springstubb
Illustrations copyright © 2015 by Gilbert Ford
All rights reserved. Printed in the United States of America.
No part of this book may be used or reproduced in any manner whatsoever without
written permission except in the case of brief quotations embodied in critical articles
and reviews. For information address HarperCollins Children's Books, a division of
HarperCollins Publishers, 195 Broadway, New York, NY 10007.
www.harpercollinschildrens.com

ISBN 978-0-06-211294-1

16 17 18 19 20   CG/OPM   10 9 8 7 6 5 4 3 2 1
❖
First paperback edition, 2016

For my antediluvian love, Paul

chapter one

Transparent. That's how Flor and Sylvie are to each other. See-through. Flor knows everything about Sylvie, and Sylvie? She knows things about Flor before Flor knows them herself.

Sylvie cheers Flor up or calms her down. Considers the same stuff funny or annoying. Won't tease her for still being scared of the dark, not to mention those spiders with hairy legs, and loves pretending their bikes are wild horses only they can tame. Sylvie, world's most awesome friend, never laughs at Flor, or if she does, it's the kind of laugh that means *oh-wow-you-are-one-of-a-kind-and-I-love-you,* never *oh-wow-how-can-anyone-possibly-be-so-weird-a-roo.*

"Best friends" does not cover it. They are each other's perfect friend.

Add this: Flor O'Dell and Sylvie Pinch live on a small island in a great lake. An island so small it's barely more than a lump of limestone. So minuscule that when the ferries shut down and the summer people leave, fewer than two hundred souls live here, and that's counting Flossie the gangster cat and Minerva the two-legged dog. Flor and Sylvie are the only eleven-year-old humans for watery miles and miles.

Think of it. How amazing, how excellent, how rare is that? In Flor's opinion, very.

But she hasn't seen Sylvie in four days. Practically a record in the lifelong history of their friendship. Sylvie has been sick, or busy, or something. Something peculiar. Something strange. Then this morning, this bright, hot July morning, she called. "Come right over," Sylvie whispered. "Right this minute."

Flor jumps on her trusty bike, bends low over the handlebars.

"Fly, Misty! Fly like the western wind!"

The morning becomes a dazzling blur. Last night it rained, and the world is polished up. The leaves on the trees are a deeper green, the rocks have lost their dust, and every dip in the land brims and winks in the sunlight. Water and rock—that's what Moonpenny Island is made of. Talk about opposites! The lake is a show-off blabbermouth. It can't stand to be ignored for a single solitary minute. Moonpenny is so little only a blind person could get lost here, though even she—the blind person—could find her way by listening for the mutters and murmurs, slaps and crashes of the water. Meanwhile, the rocks keep quiet. When Flor was in third grade and had to draw a spelling picture for *secret*, she drew a rock.

Now she rides no-handed, arms dangling. Her grandmother Lita, who lives on the mainland, has a sampler on her living room wall: GOD'S IN HIS HEAVEN—ALL'S RIGHT WITH THE WORLD! Exactly. Flor passes summer people in rented golf carts and Camp Agape campers on clunky camp bikes. Queenie from Two Sisters store, bobbing to her car radio, waves. The dark, curly head of Joe Hawkins pokes up from his family's front yard, basically a graveyard for things summer people toss. Old bikes, rusted outboards, dilapidated deck chairs—Joe's father is a junk-oholic.

"Hey, Floor." Joe waves. "Where's your sister, Ceiling?"

Once, for about three minutes, Flor and Sylvie decided Joe was cute. What were they thinking? She almost shouts back at him, then bites her tongue. When she was little, Flor was famous for her bad temper. Her big sister, Cecilia, still has a faint tattoo of Flor's baby teeth on her left arm. Now that she's older, though, Flor exercises self-control. Not that injustice, and the victimizing of the small, the weak, and the four-legged, don't enrage her still. But now she knows how to handle her anger.

Mostly.

The rain turned the lake brown and foamy as a fancy coffee drink. She glides by a few more houses, then claps her hands over her ears as she passes Pinch Paving and Stone, the last working quarry. Inside the tall barbed-wire fence, the diggers and hoppers, feeders and crushers, roar and growl. A crane like a dinosaur skeleton juts against the sky. Cutting and crushing limestone is no dainty job. Sylvie's father owns the quarry, and Sylvie hates it. She says the quarry makes her feel sorry for Mother Earth.

Crazy-tenderhearted, that's Sylvie Pinch. Once she and Flor dragged all the island's tossed-out Christmas trees back to her house, because Sylvie felt bad for them. That same Christmas, when her mother got a new toaster, Sylvie took the old one to bed with her every night for a week. Her bed was a mess of toast crumbs. If Sylvie's heart was a fruit, it would be a sweet, ripe strawberry.

Her house sits on the island's only rise. All glass and stone, it hogs up the best view of the sunset. Flor's house could fit inside twice. It's funny how, lately, Sylvie always wants to come over to Flor's. She says she likes the O'Dell house better, because it's so cozy. Which is Sylvie-speak for crowded and old.

She's waiting at the foot of her long driveway, riding her purple bike in lazy circles. The purple ties of her swimsuit—two-piece, bought by her mother from a boutique on the mainland—poke out the neck of her purple-and-white T-shirt. Her purple helmet is on her head, her purple high-tops on her feet. Both knees have Band-Aids. Beige, not purple. Though that bruise on her cheek is.

"I tripped," Sylvie says when she sees Flor's *what-happened* face. "Down the . . . the cellar steps."

"Yikes." There's another bruise on Sylvie's forehead. "Ouch."

"I know." She switches into her alien voice. "I inhabit the planet Clumsy."

The sudden spit of gravel sends them scrambling. A red SUV shoots down the drive, Sylvie's handsome, bad-news brother at the wheel.

"Slow down!" they holler at the top of their lungs, but he barely taps the brake before he rockets out into the road.

"I thought he was working at the quarry this summer," says Flor.

"He is."

"Well, he's going the exact wrong direction."

Sylvie sighs. "If only he wouldn't drive like that. It gets me so worried." She pushes her purple glasses up her nose and sighs again, and Flor wishes, not for the first time, that the Earth would yawn and swallow Peregrine Pinch IV feet first.

The Pinches' ancestors settled the island forever ago, when it still rightfully belonged to Indians. The Indians are long gone, but not the Pinches. Sylvie's family owns the ferry, the Cockeyed Gull restaurant, and of course that deafening quarry. Peregrine Pinch III, Sylvie's father, is the mayor. If the island had royalty, Sylvie's family would all wear crowns.

Perry Pinch is the prince. The spoiled rotten kind. Last month he got in a fistfight with a summer kid. The month before, he got caught stealing at Two Sisters, even though he had a pocket full of money. The month before—well, don't get Flor started.

Sylvie squints up the road, though the car's long disappeared. She loves her big brother beyond all reason. She adores that chucklehead so completely, so blindly, it could almost make a person jealous.

"My parents had a fight over Perry last night." Flor's surprised to hear herself say this, since how much her parents argue isn't high on her list of conversation topics. Too late now. Sylvie's blue eyes widen, and Flor has to explain. "My mother said my father should give him a speeding ticket, and my father said he guesses after all these years he

7

knows how to be the island cop."

"Your father never gives islanders tickets. He hardly ever even gives them to summer people."

"I know. My parents can fight over anything these days. The tiniest, most unimportant thing. It's a special talent they've developed." Flor digs gravel out of her sandal. Lately, her parents take longer and longer to make up. Lately, Dad's spending more nights on the couch, and the only time you hear Mama singing is in church. "If there was a show called *Find the Most Ridiculous Thing to Fight About*, they'd win the boat and the car and the vacation house."

"Adults are crazy-bizarre."

"We'll never be like that."

"Never."

But an odd look comes into Sylvie's eyes. Something surfaces, something Flor can't name, and it makes her heart reset its beat. What? Sylvie hops on her bike and starts pedaling.

"Where were we before we were so rudely interrupted?"

"You were falling down the cellar stairs."

"Enough of that rubbish," Sylvie says in her English-lady voice.

They gallop, leaving trouble behind. Civilization on one side, lake sparkle on the other. A birder, standing in tall grass, trains his binoculars on them. Flor and Sylvie, a rare species! Beach towels ripple on clotheslines, and in the cottage windows, curtains rise and fall. That thug of a cat, Flossie Magruder, crouches in the weeds, a doomed field mouse between her big paws. Passing the turnoff for the winery, they hear loud music and laughing, though it's barely noon. Summer people! Year-rounders turn up their noses at them. "Before they board the ferry, they leave their brains behind in a bucket," islanders say.

Summer people don't know about the swimming hole. It's hidden away in the old quarry off Moonpenny Road. Sylvie and Flor leave their bikes on the edge and scramble down the steep sides. Their feet set off mini avalanches, and they grab at scrubby juniper bushes to keep from falling. This place got quarried out years ago, and the sides are slowly silting in. Weeds and wildflowers poke through the cracks in the stony floor, and big blocks of limestone lie tumbled around. When you get to the bottom and look up, you're a Cheerio in a giant bowl, or a little fish in a great stone tank. Walk back to that papery screen of cattails, part them with both hands, step inside.

Silvery rocks, speckled with lichen, warm in the sun. The pool is so deep, so clear and cold, that the minute she sees it, Flor shivers. That water stops your breath. Every single time, it stops your breath.

Of course, they're not allowed in alone. If the island mothers had their way, NO SWIMMING ALONE would be tattooed on every child's forehead. People have drowned here, including two star-crossed lovers who loaded their pockets with stones, exchanged one last passionate kiss, and jumped in. Who would be so brainless? Another time, a girl known to be an excellent swimmer sank from view right before the eyes of her hysterical parents, who couldn't save her. Everybody says the hole has no bottom, though how can that be?

The dry cattails sway and rustle, even though there's no breeze. Flor doesn't believe in ghosts. Still, she'd rather die than be here at night. Flor's afraid of the dark, and out here, she can tell, the dark would be that thick, suffocating kind, the kind that rubs against you like black fur.

Boiling hot as she and Sylvie are, they don't dare

go in that water yet. A big toe, that's all for now.

Instead they stretch out on their favorite rock, wide and flat as a refrigerator, and open their books. Flor could read till her eyes fell out. Sylvie's never big on books, and today she can't seem to concentrate at all. She jumps up and prowls around, collecting rocks.

"How can something have no bottom?" says Flor.

"I don't know. Did you ever dream you were falling and falling and you were never going to stop?"

"Eek. No."

Sylvie's hand goes to her bruised cheek. She's on the slippery edge of the hole, sliding one long, skinny foot in front of the other. For no good reason, a chill knifes through Flor, right there in the crazy-hot sun.

"Careful!" she yells at her friend.

A nature trail rims the quarry, with boring markers describing this and that, and they can hear some clueless summer people up there, trudging through the rising heat. Sylvie arranges her rocks. Flor turns pages. A dragonfly with iridescent wings hovers over her book like it wishes it knew how to read.

"Look," says Sylvie then.

Flor raises her eyes, catches her breath. Sylvie is always building stuff, but this may be her master-piece. She's arranged the stones into a cross between a fairy castle and a cathedral. She's made turrets and towers and, at the very center, a round room paved with sparkling pebbles and slivers of slate.

"If only we knew a shrinking spell!" says Flor. "We could live there together."

Sylvie laughs. Her blond ponytail shoots up like a geyser.

"We'd drink dew and eat wild blueberries."

"Hitch rides on dragonflies."

"We'd weave dresses from spider silk."

"Not the kind with hairy legs."

"Never!"

Sylvie shows Flor the gray rock she laid on the very top. One corner has a pleat, like a tiny white fan. A fossil.

They put their foreheads together and make a wish, the way they always do when they find one.

Never parted, wishes Flor. Looking up into Sylvie's blue eyes, she knows their wishes match.

Transparent. That's how they are.

Later, a couple of mothers show up with their kids. At last, Flor and Sylvie are officially allowed in the water. They tear off their T-shirts.

Only, what's this? Poor Sylvie has yet another bruise, this one on her shoulder. Seeing Flor's face, Sylvie spins away, shouts, "Ready?"

"Ready!"

Holding hands, they count to three, then, because Flor chickened out, to five. Eyes squeezed shut, screaming to wake the dead, they leap.

The water stops their breath.

chapter two

That nursery rhyme claims little boys are made of snips and snails and puppy-dog tails, but Flor is certain her brother is ninety-nine percent dirt. Lately he spends all his time with a summer kid named Benjamin, and their main activity must be rolling on the ground. Usually Thomas follows Flor everywhere, so this development is a relief. Except for how disgustingly filthy he is.

Thomas's other new thing is whistling. This is an improvement over when he said everything in what he claimed was Martian, and definitely better than when his answer to any question was "It's complicated."

Did you brush your teeth? "It's complicated."

Why is your shirt inside out? "It's complicated."

Have you seen Dad's fishing pole? "It's . . ."

You get the idea.

At least when he's whistling, he's not talking.

Today when Flor gets home from swimming, she hears him in the bathroom, whistling softly and steadily. Carrying a tune doesn't figure in. They only have one bathroom, and Flor needs a shower. When she knocks, a two-part rising whistle answers her.

"It's me," she says. "Come out. Time's up."

Now it's one long loud note, like a policeman stopping traffic.

"This is ridiculous." She tries the doorknob. Locked. "I refuse to communicate in whistles."

The toilet flushes. The sink runs for several centuries. Yet when Thomas opens the door, his face and hands are grubby as ever. A mystery. He saunters down the hall, hands in pockets, a pudgy six-year-old whistling machine.

After her shower, Flor peers into the steamy mirror. She's diligent with the sunscreen, and pale as a cauliflower. Because she's small for her age, with dark hair like her mother and fair skin like her father, people who don't know her well often ask if she feels all right. Whenever they visit Mama's family in Toledo, Lita forces her to eat fried liver. Lita's convinced Flor has poor blood and sends her home with big jars of iron pills. All Mama's side of the family has beautiful caramel-colored skin and glossy dark hair. It's how Cecilia looks, and Thomas too. But not Flor.

Sylvie says she is unique. This is Sylvie-speak for *ugly duckling.*

Mama's in the kitchen, making dinner. She can peel and chop while gazing out the window, though this makes everyone else nervous. *Chop chop,* those carrots are goners. *Whoosh,* they cascade into the pot. She dries her hands, cocks a look at Flor.

"Fetch the comb and brush," she says.

Nothing. That's what Flor loves more than Mama French braiding her hair. Usually when Mama pays her particular, undivided attention, it's to scold her for being so stubborn, or flipping her lip, or teasing poor little Thomas. But when she's braiding Flor's hair, lifting the strands and twining them smooth,

Mama's strong fingers do the talking.

You are my girl. My one and only Flor.

No one else pronounces her name that exact way, stretching it into two emerald-green syllables, making Flor see a vine twisting up a wall, white flowers like stars. It's the way her name is meant to sound.

Just as Mama finishes, Cecilia walks in. Flor's big sister sails straight to the refrigerator.

"And where have you been all afternoon?" Mama's not really angry. Trouble? Cecilia never causes it, never gets into it.

Cecilia selects a single radish. She takes it to the sink, washes it like it's about to have surgery, and takes a bite. Who eats a radish in more than one bite? A sister who's on a diet, though she will never admit it.

"You were at the library again," Mama accuses. "Don't think you can fool me."

Mama frets Cecilia doesn't have enough friends, and this is true, though it's not Cele's fault. Besides Perry Pinch IV, the island school has four other high schoolers, and none of them even remotely qualifies as a good, let alone perfect, friend. Once upon a time, Cele and Flor played together. They invented so many excellent games! Town—that was their best. Good old Town. Let it be said that Flor was not the one to put an end to that.

"I'm getting a head start on chemistry." Cecilia nibbles her radish. "Considering Mrs. Plum probably doesn't know a molecule from a mole, and I'll mainly have to teach myself."

"But," begins Flor, and her big sister shoots her the death ray. The words *The library isn't open today* vaporize.

"It's a whole month till school. *¡Dios mío!*" scolds Mama. "Plenty of time to study!"

Cecilia circles her arms around their mother, rests her chin on Mama's shoulder. She's always been prettier than Flor, but lately? Her dark eyes are bright, her hair shiny as a waterfall. A person would think she was in love, and she probably would be, if she lived anywhere else. Moonpenny has everything a person could dream of, Dad always says. Of course, he doesn't dream of having a boyfriend.

"Whoever heard of a mother discouraging her kid from studying?" Cele says. "You're *loca*! My *mamacita loca*."

Over Mama's shoulder, she smiles at Flor. Lately, Cecilia has become a real smile miser, so this is a surprise. It should make Flor suspicious. Instead, her foolish mouth votes to smile back.

Dad's late for dinner, highly unusual. He is a police officer. *The* police officer. He drives a beat-up SUV with a mail-order clip-on light and carries a gun he's never once shot, except at the targets behind the VFW. In summer, Dad's job is fishing water snakes out of nervous ladies' rain barrels and tipsy tourists out of the lake. Winters, he checks on closed-up cottages, settles late-night arguments at the Cockeyed Gull. Now and then Thomas wishes for a big car chase or a wild shoot-out, like on TV, but Thomas is only six, plus a boy, so what can you expect.

Flor is grateful their father's job isn't dangerous. And she's proud of him. Everyone on the island likes Dad, except when they don't, and that's always because they did something they shouldn't have and got caught. Getting caught is guaranteed, on Moonpenny.

Today he's gone out to check on old Violet

Tinkiss, who lives alone. Dad makes sure Violet and her two-legged dog, Minnie, have food and her roof's not leaking too bad.

No way that should take this long. Mama's fussing over her dried-up chicken frijoles when tires crunch the gravel driveway. Dad comes in and collapses into a kitchen chair. He looks terrible. Thomas sounds an alarmed whistle.

"What happened?" cries Mama. "Where were you?"

Dad is big. His dangling arms practically touch the floor.

"Accident," he says. "Out by the neck. That fool Perry Pinch flipped his car."

"Oh, no!" everybody cries—everybody except Cecilia, who goes statue still. "Is he all right? How did it happen? Was there another car?"

Flor remembers how she and Sylvie hollered at him to slow down. Sylvie! Poor Sylvie. She'll die if anything happens to her brother.

"He'll be okay," says Dad. "Looks like he broke his arm and bruised a couple of ribs. Perry Senior is flying him over to Toledo General. The car's totaled. He must've been going like a bat out of you-know-where, on that narrow, winding road." Dad runs his hand from the back of his head to the front. His reddish-brown hair leaps to attention. "At least he didn't have anyone with him. The passenger side was stove in."

Cecilia starts crying, so quietly only Flor notices.

"Was he drinking?" Mama's hands fly to her hips.

"Could be."

"You didn't do the test?" Mama's voice whittles to a point.

"Now what'd be the good of that?" Dad pulls at the skin under his jaw. "Trust me, that boy has learned his lesson."

"Just like I was saying last night! He could've hit someone! What if a child was in the road?"

Mama would've made a good lawyer or judge, the kind who throws people in jail for life. Thomas gives a *here-they-go* whistle and crawls under the table. The tears roll down Cecilia's cheeks faster than she can wipe them away.

"Well, he didn't," says Dad. "And Perry Senior's not likely to let him drive again anytime soon."

"That boy needs to suffer some real consequences."

"He's suffering, guaranteed," says Dad. "Cracked ribs are no joke."

Dad never starts these arguments, so far as Flor can see. And once they get started, he tries to end them as quickly as possible. A mistake. When's he going to realize that only makes Mama angrier? When's Mama going to realize he is who he is?

"Smells great, Bea." He lifts the lid from the skillet, trying to distract her. "I'm so hungry I could eat my own arm."

"The law goes for everyone. Including the almighty Pinches."

"There's extenuating circumstances," says Dad.

"If his parents won't punish him, the law needs to step in."

Dad carefully replaces the lid. He was born and raised here. Being the island cop is his lifelong dream come true. Taking the job to heart does not begin to cover it. Under the table, Thomas starts to whistle, then thinks better of it. Dad's voice cracks the silence.

"If you're saying I'm shirking my duty, Beatriz, I'd appreciate an apology."

"What I'm saying—" Mama begins.

But now a spoon arrows through the air between them. It bounces off the refrigerator and clatters to the floor.

"I can't believe you two are arguing over this! You're heartless and cruel. Beyond heartless and cruel!"

Cecilia pounds up the stairs. *Slam!* It's a wonder her bedroom door doesn't fly off the hinges. In the kitchen, no one moves. Flor's the one who makes big stinks, not Cecilia. Mama stares at nothing, then grabs a spoon and starts dishing out dinner. Creeping out from under the table, Thomas digs in, but Dad says he needs a shower, and no way can Flor eat now.

"I have to go see Sylvie," she says, and though Mama believes skipping a family meal is a sin against God, she nods.

Flor swings into the saddle and flies down the road, Misty's mane streaming. Up that long steep driveway, horse and girl as one. Mrs. Pinch half opens the door.

"Oh, hello, Flor."

Her mother—that's where Sylvie and her brother got their looks. But tonight she seems exhausted. And she smells funny, sweetness layered on top of bitterness.

"Is Sylvie . . ."

Mrs. Pinch shakes her head. She doesn't bother to tell Flor what happened because by now, word's out all over the island. News here travels at approximately the speed of light.

"She begged so hard to go along to the hospital, her father gave in."

"Oh."

Mrs. Pinch will never win any warm-and-friendly contests, and right now it's plain the one thing she wants in this world is to shut that door. But Flor sticks her foot in the crack.

"I'm glad Perry's going to be okay," she says.

"Thank you."

"Tell Sylvie to call me, okay?"

"It won't be till tomorrow. If then."

"But whenever."

Mrs. Pinch special orders cosmetics and beauty products, flown in by Island Air. Flor thinks her anti-wrinkle cream must not be working—she looks older than last time Flor saw her. But then, Flor hasn't seen her up close in how long? Pretty much the entire summer, since Sylvie always wants to go to Flor's house.

"I'll tell her," says Mrs. Pinch.

"And tell her—"

The door shuts.

The sun's almost down, the lake a dull shade of gray. Woodsmoke from the campground floats on the air. Why does that smell always make a person feel lonesome? When Flor pictures Sylvie in a brightly lit, scrubbed hospital, her friend seems farther away than ever. Their afternoon together feels like last year, at least.

That odd look that came into Sylvie's eyes—it creeps back to haunt Flor. What did it mean?

Misty stumbles, snapping Flor's head forward, and just like that, she knows. *I've got a secret.* That's what the look said. *You don't get it.*

Impossible! Transparent. Just-washed windows. That's how she and Sylvie are to each other.

She has to stop by the side of the road to calm herself down. Clouds scud in, wrecking the sunset. *Slap slap slap* goes the lake, teasing and bullying the silent rocks.

Digging in the pocket of her shorts, she pulls out

the fossil Sylvie set on the tip-top of their quarry castle. Flor swiped it, just before they left. Now, in the dusky light, the white fan seems to glow with its own light. She rubs it with her thumb and makes her wish again.

chapter three

Some things in life change wham-bam, dramatic and sudden as a pin and a balloon.

But usually, change is sneakier. More like that balloon leaking its air, deflating bit by bit. For instance, Moonpenny Island, at the end of the summer season. First, a cottage or two gets shuttered up, Camp Agape pulls in its dock, fewer cars roll off the Friday-evening ferry. But the sun still pours down, and Mama still works at the gift shop, selling salt and pepper shakers shaped like lighthouses and sweatshirts that say MOONPENNY ISLAND—WHAT MORE COULD YOU WANT?

Then the clouds smother the sun, and the temperature dips, and the fudge lady decides it's time to head to Florida. Her pulling in her flag and setting out the CLOSED sign is some secret signal, because now the leaking starts for real. You can practically hear it, *hiss hiss*. One cottage after another, shut up tight. The chicory fades and the Queen Anne's lace folds itself into spindly little baskets. Fewer fishing boats go out—fewer than ever, since the algae was bad again this year, and the walleye and pike aren't what they used to be. Two Sisters quits stocking fancy food. And at Sunday Mass, lots of empty pews. Father Park heaves a sigh when he sees the collection basket.

Flor always used to love this time of year. It's her island, after all—hers and Sylvie's and their families'. They just let the summer people borrow it for a while. The pulling back, the dwindling down and burrowing in—she's always loved it. Dad says that proves she's a born and bred islander. Who needs the rest of the world? That's his philosophy.

Still. Late last winter, when the lake was good and frozen, Flor stepped out on the ice and found herself having a peculiar thought. She could walk to the mainland if she wanted. That made her remember a show she'd seen, about the first creatures to haul themselves out of the goopy prehistoric water and live on land. They resembled a cross between a fish and a lizard, neither this nor that, with beady eyes and stumpy fin legs. Not what anyone would call attractive. Yet Flor was impressed. It wasn't every day a creature did something that dramatic. That risky.

Standing on the ice that afternoon, she wondered what it'd be like to walk out and stand in the middle of the lake, equal distances from the island and the mainland, the familiar and the untried new. Like a lizard-fish deciding, *Should I go for it?* She slid a little farther out, testing, but suddenly the ice groaned and she freaked and raced back to shore.

Anyway. This coming winter, one major thing will be different. For third, fourth, and fifth grade, she and Sylvie have sat in the same classroom, first as the youngest kids, then the middle, finally the oldest. This year, they'll move into the sixth, seventh, eighth grade, taught by the infamous, the dreaded, Mrs. Defoe. Mrs. Defoe wears brown. Exclusively. She assigns six-hundred-word book reports and makes you memorize the Gettsyburg Address, though who lives there remains a mystery. She is so old, both Sylvie's and Flor's fathers had her, and Dad still pretends to shiver in fear whenever he sees her. Sylvie, who never does well in school, refuses to even speak Mrs. Defoe's name. All summer, school has been banished as a topic of conversation.

And then, wham-bam, pin to the balloon. All of a sudden, school is all they talk about.

Because it turns out Sylvie is going away. To private school on the mainland. She's going to live with her aunt and uncle, whose kids are in college now.

How can it be? It can't be.

"You know my parents have talked about it forever," says Sylvie. "They think I'd do better in private school."

"Parents talk about all kinds of stuff they'll never really do!"

"I know, but—"

"Sylvie! You didn't even tell me you applied!"

"It happened so fast. After Perry cracked up the car . . ." Sylvie pushes her purple glasses up her nose.

She folds her hands in her purple lap. They're sitting on the Pinches' private beach, a crescent of sand across the road from the house, and they're wearing matching T-shirts they got years ago, with pictures of wild horses. Sylvie's voice is flat, as if she's reciting the times tables. Which she was always terrible at. "My mother says if only Perry had gone to a better school, he would've realized his . . . what do you call it?"

"Potential?"

"Umm-hmm."

Their T-shirts are too small, especially for Sylvie, who is growing in ways Flor's not. She keeps tugging hers down in front. Flor flops backward on the sand, catapults up.

"I don't see what Perry's got to do with you." She's refusing to accept this. She's positive she can stop it. She will save Sylvie. "You don't get in trouble! You're realizing your potential just fine right here."

"If you don't count almost failing math. And being slow in reading. And . . ."

"You're not slow! You're careful."

"Mrs. Halifax didn't want to make Daddy mad. That's the only reason she passed me."

"That's not true!" Well, maybe it is. But that's not the point here. Flor rushes on. "The past is not the point. This year we're moving on. You can start fresh. But that's not even the point either!"

It's disturbingly un-Sylvie to sit so still.

"We'll change your parents' minds, don't worry." Flor is getting angrier by the second. "They're just confused. Perry wrecking the car threw them for a loop. Parents get deluded very easily."

"My father says the way I like to build stuff, I could be an architect. But you have to know math." Sylvie palms pebbles, starts to make a tiny tower. "He says at Ridgewood Academy, they teach to the individual. Whatever that means. He says I'll blossom and bloom."

"Delusion! You're already the blossoming-est, blooming-est girl in the world! Besides, do you even want to be an architect?"

"Maybe." Sylvie carefully chooses another pebble. "I don't know. I hate when people ask what I want to be."

"I know! Grown-ups always want an answer, even when there isn't one! Like remember when you had that doll with the yellow yarn hair, and you carried it around everywhere, you loved it so much, and people would always ask you, 'What's your dolly's name?'"

Sylvie balances a splinter of driftwood atop her dainty tower.

"And you wouldn't answer," Flor goes on, "because you didn't even care about a name for her. Her name was not the point."

"But one day," says Sylvie, "one day you told Mrs. Magruder, 'Her name is Bernadette.'"

"What? I don't remember that."

"In a really loud voice, you said it." A pause. "I remember thinking, 'But she's my doll. And Bernadette is an ugly name.'"

"I must've been trying to stand up for you. Were you mad at me?"

"Oh, Flor. That was back in the mists of time."

Bonk. Sylvie knocks over the tower. Pebbles fly. Flor is shocked. Not only does Sylvie remember something she can't, but Sylvie's still upset about it, Flor can tell. Suddenly they can't look at each other. They get busy watching a cormorant, a waterbird so big and heavy only its scrawny neck and head show above the surface. Submarine birds, Thomas calls them. They're so greedy, such expert fishers, the human fishermen call them way worse names.

This is weird. Flor wonders if Sylvie sees the same bird she does. All at once, she can't be 100 percent sure what her best friend is seeing through those purple-rimmed glasses.

But that doesn't change the truth. Which is: Sylvie is terrible at standing up for herself. She *does* need Flor to do it for her.

Zoop. Lightning fast, the cormorant dives and disappears. Automatically, Sylvie and Flor start counting out loud. "One Mississippi, two Mississippi . . ." They get all the way to thirty-five before the bird comes back up. Not a record, but pretty good.

All of a sudden, something thunks Flor in the center of her chest. An invisible fist, on the end of a long invisible arm.

"Sylvie."

"What?"

"How come you didn't tell me before?" All of a sudden, Flor knows: this is the point. "I mean, you applied weeks ago, right?"

"But it was way past the deadline and I have terrible grades and who knew if they'd let me in." She tugs her T-shirt down for the gazillionth time. "I bet Daddy bribed them. He probably said he'd make a big donation or something."

A few years ago, some summer people tried to prove that Pinch Paving and Stone was polluting the water supply. They had samples from a lab that proved it. But Mr. Pinch brought in his own certified crew of experts, who produced their own samples. The water quality was excellent, they said. Before you knew it, that was that. Mayor Pinch pretty much got his way in the world.

At last Sylvie meets Flor's eyes. "How could I tell you? Telling you would mean it's really going to happen."

"It's not! It can't!"

Flor pulls Sylvie to her feet. They both windmill their arms around. The faded, ghostly horses on their matching shirts leap up and down.

"You're not going! It's not fair! It's unjust! You have to tell them no. You refuse. No! You will not go. No!"

"Oh, Flor! You think I didn't already try that?

Like over and over?"

But the way Sylvie says this gives Flor another knock. Right in the same place, where she already has a bruise from the first one. And when she tries to look her best friend in the eye again, Sylvie's arms fall to her side. Her ponytail droops. She takes off her purple glasses and turns away, pretending to clean them with the hem of her too-small shirt.

"If you go, I'll be the whole entire sixth grade," says Flor.

"I know. I'm sorry."

"I'll be all alone with Joe Hawkins and Mary Long, who all she can ever talk about is her disgusting allergies."

"Flor. I can't help it."

"I'll be so alone, I might as well jump in the swim hole and drown myself right now."

Sylvie doesn't speak. Flor reads her mind, right through the back of her blond head. *This isn't just about you, Flor O'Dell.*

That makes Flor feel rotten. Rotten to the core. She picks up the biggest rock in sight and hurls it into the water.

"It's all your brother's fault." Another rock, another and another. She's a rock-hurling machine. "If he wasn't a stupid mess-up who crashed his stupid car because he's so stupid, this never would have happened!"

Even as Flor spits out the words, she knows they're not really fair. But they feel good. She hurls another rock. Like the world is fair! Out of breath, she waits for Sylvie to stick up for her beloved brother. Flor is dying to argue, dying to yell her head right off her shoulders.

Instead Sylvie just slips her glasses back on and crosses the road to her house. The house of the almighty, the royal Pinches, where all the curtains are pulled and nothing stirs. Head down, one purple high-top in front of the other, she climbs the steeply sloped, perfectly groomed lawn and opens the front door. Flor can feel in her own bruised chest the soft click that door makes as it closes.

chapter four

Usually the Pinches travel to and from the mainland in their private plane. But not today. Their car on the two-o'clock ferry, that's how Sylvie's leaving for school.

There's so much stuff, she and Flor can't both fit in the packed car. Mr. Pinch drives it to the ferry landing while the two of them follow on their bikes. Slowly. Glaciers would be like race cars next to them.

Since they knew for positive Sylvie was going, they've had a million sleepovers at Flor's, and two million picnics at their secret spot on the back shore, and three million bike rides on their valiant, spirited steeds, but so what. They still can't believe it.

The *Patricia Irene* plows the bay, looming bigger by the second. Mr. Pinch paces beside his brand-new car, replacement for the one Perry Junior wrecked. Sylvie's father is the kind of man you feel you should salute. He wears hard, shiny shoes at all times, and his forehead is so immense, he might have an extra brain in storage.

"You took long enough!" he says.

"Sorry, Daddy," says Sylvie, and all the starch goes out of him. He gives her shoulder a squeeze and smiles at Flor.

Who absolutely refuses to smile back.

Sylvie puts her purple bike in the bike rack. She's not bringing it. Her aunt and uncle have a garage full of bikes, and besides, she'll be taking a bus to school now. Ridgewood Academy. Acres of green lawns, buildings out of Harry Potter, with smiling, handsome students who loll around under trees all day, mesmerized by their smiling, handsome teachers. Sylvie and Flor have looked at online pictures of the place till their eyes fell out.

The *Patricia Irene* grinds her gears, slowing down. Mr. Pinch takes Sylvie's backpack.

"Good God!" he says. "What's in here? Rocks?"

Sylvie smiles and whispers to Flor. "I went to the quarry yesterday."

Examining the Ridgewood website, she and Flor both noticed the same thing. Not a rock in sight. Everything was lush and yielding, gently rolling, the exact opposite of this stubborn, craggy place.

Tears prick Flor's eyes. But she will not cry. No crying. She and Sylvie have a solemn pact.

Last-minute cars are pulling up, getting in line. Here comes a van, bikes on the roof, fishing poles jutting out a window. Its door slides open, and who should tumble out but Thomas. He grabs the door handle and rolls it shut with all his six-year-old might, then just stands there, toeing the gravel.

The head of his dirt-loving summer friend, Benjamin, pops out the window. His family must be leaving today too.

By now Flor can make out the faces of the ferry passengers. Mostly they're year-rounders coming back. But up on the top deck, all by herself, is a girl in a ridiculous sweatshirt. It flaps around her knees and covers her hands, plus she's got it pulled up over her nose and mouth, so pretty much all you see of her is her work boots, her eyes, and a frizz of hair wafting in the breeze. Very strange. Very peculiar.

The cars on the ferry and the ones waiting to board all start their engines. *Rmm rmm, rev rev!* What's the hurry? Why do adults make such a colossal deal out of being exactly on time? You'd think driving on or off a ferry at the precise moment the ferry guy waves his stupid flag was a matter of life or death.

Flor rolls her eyes at Sylvie. Who nods, like *I know.* That's when it hits Flor for real and true. Who's she going to talk to now? Who will understand her even when she doesn't say a word? Nobody, that's who.

The solemn pact is in great danger.

"What's in all those bags and boxes anyway?" Flor bursts out. "It looks like you packed for forever."

Sylvie's blue eyes swim with tears, and Flor bites her dumb tongue. Why's she scolding Sylvie? What's wrong with her? She reaches in her pocket and pulls out the surprise.

"Look."

Of course Sylvie remembers. The second she sees it, she knows precisely what it is.

"That day at the swimming hole!" She wipes her eyes, reaches for the rock with its delicate white fan fossil. "You took it."

"So I did."

"Should we make another wish? Do you think it works twice on the same one?"

Really, it will be wish number three, but Flor doesn't tell Sylvie that.

"If we do it at the exact same time," she assures her friend.

"On the count of three."

"One Mississippi, two Mississippi, three Mississippi . . ."

Every cell in her body, that's what Flor uses to wish. But when she opens her eyes, Sylvie's looked away. Like she's already done wishing. Or like her wish already came true.

Thunk! goes Flor's heart. No, it's the snout of the *Patricia Irene*, bumping the dock. The seagulls perched on the pilings flap their wings, annoyed. The boat ramp goes down, the thick chain gets unhooked, the flag guy waves. One by one, the cars roll onto land.

Flor slips the fossil back into her pocket. Inside her a pressure is building, pushing against her edges till any second she'll explode. Pieces of her will fly in every direction, leaving nothing except a small, sooty stain where she once stood.

Perry Pinch IV is nowhere in sight. Sylvie hasn't even mentioned that despicable boy, not once.

"Hey, you two." Mrs. Pinch leans out the car window. She's wearing even more makeup than usual. Her face is like a cake with so much icing, you get sickish halfway through. "Sylvie's not going to Outer Mongolia. You two can email and phone! And it'll be Thanksgiving before you know it."

The ignorance of grown-ups is so painful Flor has to look away, just as a golf cart rolls by. A Santa look-alike, only skinny, is at the wheel. Beside him sits that girl, huddled into her cocoon of a sweatshirt. She stares at Flor so hard, you'd think she had X-ray vision.

"Sylvie!" Mr. Pinch's voice makes them jump. "Get in this car!" The cars waiting to board begin moving forward. Sylvia trembles but doesn't move. "Sylvie Pinch!" It is the voice of a Man Who Is Obeyed. "Right this second!"

Sylvie grabs Flor's arm.

"You have to promise me something," she says. "You won't want to, but you have to."

"I want to! I will! What?"

"Look out for my brother."

Flor stares. *What?* How in the world is she supposed to do that? Perry is wild. He's big trouble. He hasn't said more than two words to her in years.

Plus she hates him.

"Sylvie!" hollers her father. People turn to look. The mayor is speaking! "Now! Right now!"

"But Syl—your father. He'll look out for Perry." How can a Pinch possibly need help from Flor? The Pinches have everything going for them.

Sylvie's eyes brim. So much for their solemn pact. It's impossible, but Flor's already-broken heart breaks even more.

"Don't worry. I'll do it." And though she's got no idea how or why, she says, "I promise. I swear on our fossil."

Sylvie hugs Flor hard, then fits herself into the Sylvie-sized space in the backseat. All those boxes and suitcases—if only Flor could stow away inside one! The pressure inside her is going in reverse, tightening into a dark solid weighing a million pounds.

Everything moves in reverse now—the ramp pulled in, the chain hooked up. The *Patricia Irene* blasts her horn and now there's water, churned up and ugly, between the ferry and the island. All the seagulls lift off at the very same moment—how do they do that? They follow the boat, swooping and squawking. Benjamin the Dirt Boy flings bits of bread, and they snatch it midair.

Where is she? Are her parents actually holding her prisoner in the car? But no, there, up on the top deck, frantically waving her arms. Flor waves back as the ferry shrink-shrink-shrinks, to the size of a toy boat, to just the idea of a boat.

Just the idea of a friend.

How do people, immigrant people, ever say good-bye to their families and everything they love and move to a strange new place? How do they stand it? It must tear them to pieces! And then she thinks, Mama's parents did. And when Mama left the mainland to live here, she sort of did. And then Flor thinks, Maybe you get used to saying good-bye. But then she thinks, Not me. Without Sylvie, Flor's world has shrunk down to her parents, brother, and sister. She's got no one else to spare. If she had to lose anybody else . . .

"I would die," she whispers.

"We'll see about that," says someone beside her.

Thomas. It's been so long since he spoke instead of whistled, she almost doesn't recognize his voice.

"Don't think just because your dirt-bomb friend's gone you can start hanging around me again," she tells him.

"We'll see about that." Hands in his pockets, he rocks back on his heels. Benjamin is already fading from his undeveloped brain, she can tell. Thomas is six. Plus a boy. He's all about now, and what next.

"You have no idea what heartache is," she informs him.

"We'll see about that."

"Oh, no, you don't. You are not starting that. Absolutely not."

"We'll see. . . ."

She grabs her bike and jumps on.

She rides bareback, fingers twined in Misty's thick mane, fast, taking the first turn, faster. Airport Road skims the east edge of the island, and she gallops past the miniature runway, past the bug-infested nature preserve, past the turn to the windswept neck where old Violet Tinkiss lives. Flor keeps her head down, partly so Misty won't hit a bump or hole, but mostly because who cares, who cares what she's passing? Who cares about anything?

The sudden honk of a horn shoots her heart into her throat. She skids onto the side of the road as a pickup barrels by. PINCH PAVING AND STONE says the side, and guess who's driving. Which he's absolutely forbidden to do, which he's doing the very minute his parents leave, which is now Flor's responsibility since she promised Sylvie she'd watch out for him . . .

"Stop!" She shakes her fist, so furious she can't see straight, can't know if she sees what she thinks she sees, which is someone in the passenger seat sliding down out of sight.

47

chapter five

Tomorrow. School starts tomorrow.

Cecilia's been in her room all day. Her domain, that's what school is. Name an award, Cecilia O'Dell has won it. You could paper a wall with all the photos of her accepting certificates and trophies and plaques. When Flor peeks in, she expects to see her sister hunched over her desk, pre-studying, but instead Cecilia lies on her bed, eyes closed and arms flung over her head, like she just fell from the sky.

"Cele?"

"Uh-huh."

"I need to ask you something."

"Uh-huh."

Flor creeps into the room. It's the size of a closet, which it was, till Cecilia wore down Dad with her pleading not to share a room with Flor anymore, and he somehow bumped out a wall and added a tiny window. It smells like nail polish and hair product in here, but also like freshly sharpened pencils and brand-new notebooks. Cecilia's desk looks like she lined things up with a ruler. Flor sighs, remembering their favorite old game, Town. Cecilia, the mayor, sat writing proclamations. Flor got to be the doctor, the store owner, the beauty-salon lady. Thomas would beg to play, and they'd hand him the wastebasket and tell him he was the garbageman, which he actually liked.

"Did you ever make a promise you couldn't keep?"

Cecilia props herself up on an elbow. She's put something on her eyes that makes them look smoky and mysterious. *Mysterious* is not a word anyone normally associates with Cecilia. *Trustworthy. Polite. Adult-friendly.* These are your common Cecilia words.

"No," says this dark stranger.

"Oh."

"I'm the exception. Lots of people break their promises. Probably most people. Toothpicks! They break promises like toothpicks."

Is this supposed to make Flor feel better or worse?

"The trick is to be choosy what you promise." Cecilia rolls onto her back again. Her glamorous eyes regard the ceiling, and she smiles, like she can see straight through to the heavens above. Flor looks up, straining to see what her sister does, but it's just that same looping crack in the ceiling, the one they call the butt crack. "Think," says Cecilia, "can I really do this? Do I want to do this, even on pain of death?"

Death? Who's talking about *death*?

"What if it's too late?" Flor says. "What if you already promised something and now you can't do it?"

"What did you promise?"

"Never mind," says Flor.

"Then never mind back."

She should've known better. When was the last time Cecilia helped her with anything besides her math, and remember what an excruciating experience

50

that was? On the way out, Flor palms some nail polish.

"Put that right back," says Cecilia without turning her head.

That night, in honor of back to school, Mama takes special requests. Thomas gets naked spaghetti. Flor gets hamburger tacos. Cecilia gets a salad, though it's common knowledge her true favorite is an oozy cheese omelet. Last month they took a shopping trip to the mainland, and their new clothes are at the ready.

Also in honor of back to school: no arguing.

Not until the three of them are in bed, anyway. Then Mama can't understand what Dad was thinking when he spent their own money for repairs on the SUV, instead of charging it to the village. Dad says he'll get the money back eventually. Thomas already grew out of the shoes they bought him last month, and he's going to need a new winter coat, Mama says, and try saying "eventually" to their credit card statement. Her voice rises. Dad's sinks.

When Thomas shows up in her bedroom doorway, Flor lifts her sheet and he climbs in.

"You can't help how fast you're growing," she tells him.

Thomas sucks the ear of Flor's favorite stuffed animal, Snowball the bunny, and she lets him. According to Cecilia, their parents didn't always fight. They met when they were really young, when Dad was still a rookie and Mama came over to work for the summer as a counselor at Camp Agape. Sparks flew, Cecilia says, and wedding bells rang. She says that she and Mama, their hair brushed to a shine and perfume dabbed behind their ears, would sit on the porch waiting for Dad to get home. Cele claims to remember when Dad tried to learn Spanish, though this sounds so preposterously un-Dad, Flor bets she made it up. Being born first puts a person in charge of the story. In Cecilia's story, small, fierce Mama and big, easygoing Dad fell in love because opposites attract. It's true that, when they're being lovey-dovey, Dad will slip his arm around Mama and say, "You can't map the ways of the heart."

Maps change, though. The one in their classroom was so outdated, Mrs. Halifax had to cross out the names of some countries and write in their new ones.

When Thomas falls asleep, Flor rescues poor Snowball. She dries and fluffs his long ears. Thomas can hog a whole bed. Another of his questionable talents. On the sliver of mattress left to her, Flor tosses and turns. Last night on the phone Sylvie said her aunt and uncle sing duets in the car and garden together on Saturdays. They call each other Pal. Weird-a-roo, said Flor. Sylvie claims they're nice. Well, who *doesn't* Sylvie say that about?

She starts school tomorrow too. Her sixth grade has one hundred kids in it. One hundred times more than Flor's.

The stairs creak. Mama. Mama alone. It's the couch for Dad again tonight.

Out Flor's window, a flash of heat lightning bleaches the sky. One time she and Sylvie threw all their Barbies out that window into the big lilac bush below. Why? A mystery. Another time they wrote love notes to Joe Hawkins and paid Thomas two dollars to slide them under his front door, then raced after him and paid him another whole dollar not to. On their first day of kindergarten, they held hands the entire time except for going to the bathroom. At the end of the day, they couldn't even unbend their fingers.

They thought that's how it would be all the way through twelfth grade. Maybe they would even go to the same college. They'd marry brothers and live on the same street.

Flor never has bad dreams, but it's possible she does that night. When she wakes up, her legs feel weak and crumply. Like she's spent hours balancing on a narrow sliver of something, and not just her own mattress.

chapter six

Moonpenny School was built back in the day, when the island had several working quarries, vineyards, family farms, and a fishing industry. Back then, armies of kids lived here. The school is three stories high, with a clock tower and everything. As long as Flor can remember, that clock has said 11:16.

This morning, seventeen kids show up, the precise same number as last year, because a new kindergartner, Jocelyn Hawkins, takes Sylvie's place. Not that anyone can. Jocelyn shadows her brother, Joe, chewing on the strap of her beat-up camouflage backpack.

She's the only girl Hawkins, and stuck wearing hand-me-down T-shirts with pictures of football players. Mr. Hawkins, their father and the school custodian, leans against the toolshed like he's already exhausted, even though it's just the first hour of the first day. At least once a month, Dad hauls Mr. Hawkins's golf cart out of some ditch he drove into on his way home from the Cockeyed Gull. Certain people—well, pretty much every adult except Dad, whose job is to look out for each and every islander, no matter what—consider the Hawkins family certified trash.

If Sylvie was here, they'd be discussing how ridiculous Joe looks with his curly hair long as a rock star. They'd be watching him toss that rock from hand to hand, scowling up at the frozen clock. Queenie's grandson Duke races past, chasing a pop fly hit by Barney Magruder. He steps on Flor's toe and doesn't even notice. She has gone invisible. Mary Long hunches by the door, nose running, clutching a box of tissues. Thomas shinnies up the flagpole. If he tears those new pants, Mama will fry him.

The high schoolers clump near the door. One, two, three, four. Where is that Perry Pinch? Late on the first day? By now he's all healed up from the accident, so what is his excuse?

Not a Pinch in sight.

Cecilia, wearing that new, clingy red sweater, which is not her style at all, looks anxious too. Odd. Very odd. At school Cecilia normally has one of two expressions: bored or fake earnest. Once, as they lay side by side staring up at the ceiling butt crack, she told Flor that she's not nearly as intelligent as everyone thinks. The island just doesn't provide a statistical sampling big enough for comparison, she said, sounding so smart she proved herself wrong. The closest Cecilia can come to a friend is Lauren Long, who calls Cecilia stuck up behind her back, but what can you expect? Lauren is a disappointed person. For one, she dreams of being a famous singer, but her voice is sandpaper, and for another, she's been in love with Perry Pinch since third grade. Ha! Guess who Perry is in love with? Himself. The one and only.

Where is that chucklehead?

Mrs. Defoe stands on the school steps, arms folded like she's posing for a statue titled *Figure of Authority*. Moonpenny School is too small to have a

57

real principal, so Mrs. Defoe is in charge. She wears a brown skirt and beige blouse. Brown shoes with brown laces. Her entire wardrobe is some shade of mud, which drove Sylvie, lover of color, insane. Even Dad swears he can't remember her ever wearing anything but. Mrs. Defoe is a human version of the frozen clock. Which, Dad likes to point out, is right twice a day.

Invisible Flor turns back toward her sister and all of a sudden remembers last night's dream. She stood perched on a ledge of smooth, slick stone, the kind by the swim hole. She couldn't see the ground. She couldn't see her feet. She couldn't see anything at all. Only darkness. *Open your eyes!* she told herself, her dream heart racing. *You're not blind—your eyes are just closed!*

Then what? Flor's real, undreaming heart quickens as she tries to remember. Did she fall? Leap? Of course she didn't leap! Into thin, treacherous nothingness? Even in her dreams she's not that *loca*!

Across the schoolyard, Cecilia's brow creases. She plucks at her new, sexy sweater like it's giving her a rash. Flor would run and grab her hand. *Are you all right?* she would ask. *Did you have a bad dream too?*

But Mrs. Defoe lifts her handbell and *clang!* The new year begins.

It's different. Everything. The room. The teacher. Being the youngest in the group again. Three eighth graders, two seventh graders, and her.

The desk next to Flor is empty.

"Welcome to the sixth grade, Flor O'Dell."

Mrs. Defoe hands her a pile of textbooks. Flor opens the one on top and sees CECILIA O'DELL written in precise, pointy letters.

"You labor in a long shadow."

Flor nods.

"Please write your name clearly and legibly. Handwriting is not a lost art in my classroom."

Flor nods again. A bobblehead, that's what she's been reduced to.

"You're a middle grader now. Expect great things of yourself, and great things will inevitably follow."

One seat over, Joe Hawkins pretends to strangle himself. Surprise and gratitude bubble up inside Flor.

And there you have the best part of the entire dreary morning.

At recess, Flor stares at a book she grabbed on the

way out. Total mesmerization, that's what she's hoping for. Unfortunately, the book turns out to be about the water cycle. She's rifling pages, searching for a single one with conversation, when she feels someone's eyes on her. She raises her head. A repeat of the morning scene. She is invisible. Still 11:16, insists the clock.

But the saying "I feel someone's eyes on me" is precise. It's like stepping into a shadow. You feel it move over you, even though you can't touch it.

Across the road, a low stone wall rings a graveyard. *The* graveyard. The Pinch family monument rises up in the center, a castle surrounded by peasant huts. Lilac bushes nod in the breeze. Lilacs adore Moonpenny's limey soil and grow to enormous proportions. Godzilla lilacs. One bush shakes in an unnatural way. It looks so funny Flor smiles, which makes her smile muscles exclaim, "Whoa! We thought you'd forgotten we even existed!"

"Want to play?" a small voice asks, and Flor spins around.

Jocelyn Hawkins. The sole kindergartner stares up at the sole sixth grader. She clutches a slender willow branch.

60

"I'm playing fairy ponies." She waves her golden wand. "They can fly. Mine's named Rainbow Sparkle Darling."

"Cool." Flor's so lonesome, she's tempted. Only there is such a thing as dignity. She holds up the deadly boring book. "I'm reading."

"Joe already taught me to read," says Jocelyn, like *what* is the big deal, and gallops away. When Flor looks back at the jittery lilac bush, it's motionless.

That night, Sylvie says Ridgewood Academy has groups, like the popular group and the sports group and the nerdy group, which is something they've seen on TV shows and in magazines but never for real. On Moonpenny there aren't enough kids for groups.

"And you have to pick," says Sylvie. "Or else you're in the out group."

"Which one will you pick?"

"I don't know!"

"You should go for popular."

"Then in French, the teacher only spoke French! I couldn't understand a single word. And in math they might as well have been speaking another language too. By the end of the day, I just wanted to come home. I mean, real home."

Flor's sitting in the hallway on the bottom step, her family ebbing and flowing around her. She's waiting for Sylvie to ask about her day—her long list of complaints is all prepared. First, though, Sylvie needs cheering up.

"Tell me something good." This is what Dad says to her when she's feeling blue. "There had to be at least one thing good."

"Well, the art room." Sylvie describes the tall windows and the cabinets brimming with paints and paper, and how you can learn to make jewelry or throw pots or carve wood. They even have welding supplies, to blast metal into sculptures. She goes on so long that Flor at last has to interrupt.

"Someone spied on me at recess."

"What?"

"A new kid came the day you left. On the very same ferry."

"Like reincarnation?"

"I haven't seen her since. I heard her father's a geologist or something and they're staying at the inn. Maybe it was her."

"Why would she spy? How come she doesn't have to go to school?"

They speculate as Cecilia drifts through the hallway, cell phone in hand, holding her head like a birder listening for a rare species. Even when drifting, Cecilia has perfect posture. Thomas thunders down the steps, leaps over Flor, and keeps on going. Mama yells to halt in the name of the law! Thomas tries "We'll see about that," but there's no escaping the long arm of Mama. Never, ever. Mama takes him prisoner, and he's on his way to the bathtub. Flor's fingers are going bloodless, she's been holding the phone so long.

"Flor?"

Uh-oh. Flor can hear what's coming.

"So, did you . . ."

"He ditched, Sylvie."

"What? On the first day?"

Sylvie sounds heartbroken. If that idiot Perry stood in front of Flor now, she'd pinch his head off. Ha! Pinch!

The second she hangs up, the phone rings again.

"Don't worry! If he doesn't come to school tomorrow, I'll . . ."

"Flor? It's you?"

"Oh, Lita. *Hola.*"

Her grandmother doesn't waste time on greetings but launches into a cross-examination of whether Flor is taking those iron pills, not to mention if she's studying hard in her pitiful island school. Lita and the aunts never come to Moonpenny. They act like people here live in huts and eat fish blubber. Toledo, the city—that's their idea of paradise. In the background, aunts and uncles and cousins laugh and talk, Spanish and English flitting around each other like crazy-bright butterflies. Mama's family is big, and they all live near one another. They act devastated when, after a visit, Mama packs up to return here. They act as if they thought this time for sure Mama would come to her senses and stay. Riding home to Moonpenny, where she's the only one who knows how to sing or pray in Spanish, the only one who checks anything other than Caucasian on forms, Mama stays quiet for miles and miles. Their car feels crowded with the relatives—you can almost hear their voices, almost feel their arms around you, and Flor, Cecilia, and Thomas keep quiet too, careful not to break the spell. Dad slips Mama sideways glances, his eyes apologetic. Not till the car rolls off the ferry and onto the island does Mama give her shoulders a brisk shake and start to issue orders about unpacking and chores.

Today Lita has a cold and keeps clearing her throat. When Mama takes the phone, her forehead accordions up.

"Are you sick?" she asks, immediately worried, and switches into Spanish.

Flor leans back against the stairs. So many people in this world miss other people. Cecilia drifts by again, anxiously listening for that rare birdsong, not glancing at Flor, and Flor thinks you can even miss people who are right in front of you.

That night, Flor sends Sylvie an email.

> We have to make a plan. Can you bump your head and pretend to go delusional? They'd send you home for sure.

chapter seven

Flor and Misty trot down Lilac Lane, out onto
Shore Road, past Pinch Paving and Stone. Past
the Pinches' big house, which, now that it's Sylvie-
less, makes Flor think *mausoleum*, though she's not
sure what that is. Trot into town, where Flossie
Magruder the gangster cat sits on the front steps of
the post office, licking her big paw. The last of the
fairy roses still bloom, each a perfect doll's bouquet.
A lone seagull does its goofy, backward-knee walk
along the shore. The single faithful stoplight blinks,
though there's not a car in sight. She pokes her head

into Two Sisters just to say hello. Queenie looks up from her sudoku and smiles.

"What's up?" she asks.

"The sun," Flor says.

Every time, they say this.

Flor steps back outside. An empty chip bag skips across the sidewalk and hugs her ankle like it wants company. Except for the distant din of the quarry, it's perfectly quiet. The way born and bred islanders like it. Just how they like it. Exactly.

A flock of birds streaks overhead, in a hurry to get out of town.

A few days later, Flor's once more a solitary rock in the river of recess when the graveyard lilac starts to shimmy. Tucking her book under her arm, she darts across the road.

"Hello in there."

The bush does not reply.

"You're not a very good spy. Plus, guaranteed you won't see anything much."

"I'm not spying." The voice is surprisingly deep. "And there is plenty to see."

"Really? Like what?"

"You're the one who lives here. Shouldn't you know?"

"That's rude."

"I'm not spying. I'm observing. Which, FYI, is step two in the scientific method."

"I know that. FYI, step one is pose a question. Such as, 'Why am I talking to a lilac bush?'"

Is that a laugh? Or a disgusted grunt? It's impossible to tell when gazing into branches and leaves instead of a face. Across the road, Mrs. Defoe calls her name. *"Flor!"* She makes it sound like something you walk on.

"Gotta go." Flor races back to the school yard.

"Have you forgotten the rules?" Her teacher's brown arms are crossed. Her brown toe taps. "No leaving school grounds without permission."

I was discussing the scientific method, Flor could say. Across the road, the lilac quivers. A hiking boot with red laces pokes out. Strange. Exceedingly strange. Flor has to smile.

"You're a sixth grader now. *The* sixth grader. The legacy of an entire class rests on your shoulders." The way Mrs. Defoe is positioned, the clock tower appears to jut straight out of her head. "Are your shoulders capable of that responsibility, Flor O'Dell?"

"Sorry," says Flor. "I mean, yes."

Mrs. Defoe leans forward. The clock tower is now an extension of her spine.

"I ran into Mrs. Pinch the other day." She sniffs as if detecting an unpleasant odor. "I hear Sylvie's new school is far superior in every way. Is what I hear."

"Sylvie actually hates it there."

Mrs. Defoe smiles. Smiling changes anyone's face, but hers gets a total makeover. Her twelve million wrinkles flatten, and her big teeth flash in the sun.

"Is that what she told you?"

"She'd come back in a heartbeat if she could." Maybe it's not exactly what Sylvie said. But close enough.

"She's not impressed by all those fancy bells and expensive whistles? Well, I can't say I'm surprised. Not surprised in the least. Give me the old-fashioned ways any day, and twice on Sunday."

A loud *clunk* turns them both around. Joe Hawkins just threw a rock at the clock tower. Mrs.

Defoe's face becomes a mask of horror. Can the boy have lost his mind? Yes, because look, he's picking up another rock! But before he can let it fly, a rusted-out van clanks to a halt in the parking lot, and out shambles his father. Mr. Hawkins drank his lunch at the Cockeyed Gull again—the scientific method is not required to deduce this. Joe drops the rock. He grabs his father's arm. Whatever he says makes Mr. Hawkins square his shoulders. Straighten up and grab his toolbox.

Mrs. Defoe shakes her head slowly. *Tch tch.* "He was once a promising student."

"He still is!" says Flor.

"I mean *Mr.* Hawkins." Her teacher sighs. The million wrinkles make a comeback. "He had a natural aptitude for math. He could have taught me a thing or two, believe it or not." She speaks like a person recalling something lost and precious. "But somewhere along the way . . ."

"You can't map the ways of the heart," says Flor, a statement that makes most adults smile. But Mrs. Defoe's penciled-on eyebrows shoot up.

"Teachers take their pupils' fates to heart, Flor

O'Dell. When a student squanders his God-given gifts, we see it as our own failure."

Jocelyn Hawkins, lone kindergartner, skips across the grass. She taps her father with her golden wand, then slips her hand into his. Her smile says, *You are the sun and I am a planet.* Don't try and tell Jocelyn her father is a loser.

The three Hawkinses climb the front steps, passing Cecilia, who huddles against the building with her cell phone to her ear. Her free hand's in front of her face, like she's casting a spell of invisibility. And it works. Cell phones are against school rules. But somehow Mrs. Defoe doesn't see. Somehow nobody ever sees Cecilia doing anything wrong.

Except Flor. She sees. And wishes she didn't. Because one, Cecilia never breaks rules, and two, who in the world can she be calling?

The deep voice of the lilac echoes inside Flor. *There is plenty to see. You live here—shouldn't you know that?*

"I'm not in any group," Sylvie says that afternoon on the phone.

"You're in my group. Our group. The group of you and me."

"I'm the only one with unpierced ears. And unbraces teeth. And uncool music on my iPod."

"Un is good, Sylvie. Unusual. Who wants to be like everybody else? Of course, it's a lot easier to be unusual here on good old Moonpenny, where everybody knows you, and won't judge you based on stupid superficial stuff like your ears or your—"

"Perry dropped out of school!"

Flor's heart tumbles into her shoes. Perry hasn't come to school once, but she figured he was sick, or faking he was sick, or something.

"He quit! My mother called and told me."

Flor leans against the kitchen sink. She promised to look out for him. Is this her fault? This is her fault.

"My mother wants me to talk him out of it, but he won't answer his phone." Sylvie's voice trembles. "Flor, I'm not supposed to tell anybody. Okay?"

Like they're going to be able to keep this a secret? Confused, Flor looks through the window over the sink. Cecilia's out there, lying on Mama's lounger. Flor stares at her sister, tries to think of what to say.

"Daddy's ready to kill him. He's more worried what people will say about the mayor's son being a dropout than he is about Perry. What kind of father cares more about gossip than his own son?"

Whoa. It's anti-Sylvie to criticize anyone, even her own parents. Absence is supposed to make the heart grow fonder, but it's making hers grow tougher. Flor stares out the window. Cecilia's eyes are closed, and between her fingers is a sprig of something pink. She doesn't move a muscle. Flossie Magruder, that thug of a cat, crouches in the grass, watching her.

"Flor! You're not saying anything."

"Oh. . . . I mean . . . why's he quitting?"

"He hates it. School's even harder for him than for me. Daddy says that's because he's lazy and doesn't try. Daddy says . . ." Sylvie breaks off, like she's said more than she meant to. Like there's still more she's not supposed to tell. "Anyway. Perry says everybody expects him to mess up. 'Why disappoint people?' he says."

"Perry shouldn't blame other people for his troubles." Mama's voice comes out of Flor's own mouth. "It's his fault."

Sylvie goes quiet. Not comfortable, best-friend kind of quiet. In the background, Flor can hear a barking dog and the honk of a car horn. Sylvie's outside, under the very same September sky, only now it feels like she's on another planet, hurtling around a different star. Flor turns the water on, turns it off. Out the window lies Cecilia. She looks just like Mama when Mama was a girl, Lita says.

"My mother said Perry didn't come home last night." Sylvie's voice could fit inside a thimble. "Have you seen him, Flor?"

"No." What a pathetic word. Flor toes the worn spot Mama's feet have made in front of the sink. "I'm sorry. I know I promised to look out for him."

"I bet he broke into a cottage and slept there. He does that."

"He does?"

"Don't tell your dad, okay?"

Another secret! Flor concentrates on her lifeless sister. It's like watching one of those cement lawn-ornament lighthouses Mama sells at the gift shop. Sylvie is saying Perry wants to live someplace he can drive as fast as he wants as far as he can and there's no water cutting him off from the rest of the world.

On the other side of the window, Flossie swishes her tail. Cecilia's black hair makes a curtain across her face. A leaf drifts down and lands on her thigh.

"He wants to live where nobody knows who his father is and he can be his own person. Oh, Flor!" Sylvie draws a shaky breath. "He quit school. What next? What if he runs away?"

Runs away! As soon as Sylvie says it, Flor can imagine it. Her heart starts to beat too fast. Going up on her toes, she leans toward the window. Waves of late-afternoon light shimmer around her big sister. Who lies there like a shell. Like her body's a shell and the real Cele has gone away. Has run away.

"No!" she tells Sylvie. "He won't. Don't worry. Teenagers say all kinds of chucklehead things."

How can anyone lie so still so long? How can anyone be so beautiful? It's like she's in a trance. Bewitched. Cecilia and not, at the same time. Flor's heart thumps.

"It'll be okay," she promises Sylvie, but somehow she's promising herself too. "It'll be all right."

75

"You can't promise that."

"Yes, I can! I just did!"

Flossie's ear, the one with a bite out of it, twitches like danger is near. And now something very peculiar happens. Flor has never seen a genuine dead person, but all of a sudden, she imagines her sister in her coffin. Cecilia ate the poisoned apple, or was bitten by a venomous snake, or inhaled toxic gas. There she lies, beautiful and prim as ever but dead, dead, dead.

"Oh!" Flor cries.

"What?" Sylvie says.

When Flor flings open the kitchen door, Flossie Magruder streaks off into the field. Flor rushes to her sister's side and kneels down. Cecilia doesn't move. Her thumb and first finger pinch the stem of a fairy rose.

"Cele," breathes Flor. "Open your eyes!"

"No," replies her sister.

And Flor isn't relieved, exactly, because she knew, in her heart of hearts, didn't she, that her sister wasn't really dead. But for one terrifying moment, death was so near, so real, Flor could feel its icy breath and see its clammy hands reaching for Cecilia, greedy to drag her away. Flor swivels her head as if she still might spot the wicked witch, the slithering snake or cloud of black gas. She will chase it down, she will beat it back, she will . . .

Someone gulps in her ear.

"Flor? Are you still there? Are you okay?"

Flor sinks down into the grass.

"Everything's fine," she says into the phone. "Don't worry!"

Cecilia swings her long legs to the ground and stalks away. When Flor collapses onto the lounger, its cushions are still warm from the body of her living, undead sister. Tucking the phone under her chin, she picks up the rose and starts pulling off petals.

"I know I didn't keep my first promise. But now . . ."

"It's not your fault," says Sylvie. "I need to come home! I begged my mother, at least for the weekend, but she says I have to stay and get used to it."

Get used to it! How can adults say these heartless things? "Get used to it" belongs in the same infuriating category as "Life isn't fair" and "Someday you'll laugh over this." A horrifying thing must happen to your brain as you age. It must grow tough and rubbery, like an old pork chop forgotten in the back of the refrigerator.

She and Sylvie try to formulate a plan. Running away. A hunger strike. Maybe Sylvie could do some criminal activity and get expelled.

The backyard gives way to a field, and the field runs downhill to the lake. By now the sun's low in the sky, and if Flor stays here much longer, it will sink and melt into the water. In the tall grass, a few crickets are already chirping, that slow, mournful, end-of-summer chirp, and now Flor feels worn-out. Her sister isn't dead, but she has disappeared. The odds of Sylvie running away, or refusing to eat, or spray-painting curse words on the side of a building, or rebelling in any helpful, useful way are a million to one.

"It's okay," Sylvie says. "Talking to you makes everything better."

"How can it? Nothing's changed."

"I know." Her voice is much too calm. Peculiarly calm. "But it's okay."

Flor tries to argue this makes zero sense. It's the

kind of thing grown-ups say when they're sick of a subject. At this rate, Sylvie will either spend the year in abject misery or she *will* get used to it there, and which is worse?

"Flor, don't tell anyone what I said about my father and Perry."

"Who would I tell? Are you forgetting I have no friends?"

The breeze scatters the rose petals Flor tore to smithereens. Sylvie sighs and hangs up.

Inside the house, a miracle has occurred. Thomas is doing his homework, though no one stands over him with a whip. He points to his paper.

"Look. The word *bed* looks like what it is."

He's right.

"How come all words aren't like that?" Tiny candles of discovery light his eyes. "It'd be so much better! It'd make more sense."

"I've got news. Life doesn't always make sense."

Poof. The candles go out. Thomas looks crushed. Aargh! What made her say a mean thing like that? Even if it's true? She might as well be an adult! Disgusted with herself and pretty much the universe,

79

Flor stomps around the house, which is definitely empty. No Cecilia. No Cecilia anywhere she looks.

Tonight she sends Sylvie an email suggesting they research the symptoms of highly contagious diseases. Sylvie doesn't answer.

chapter eight

Every Saturday afternoon, Dad takes shooting practice at the targets behind the VFW. He likes to keep his shooting skills sharp, just in case an escaped convict hops the ferry and holds the island hostage. After Dad does his meticulous gun-cleaning ritual, he locks his revolver away again till next Saturday.

Today his brain slips some essential gear. He suggests Thomas come target shooting with him. Thomas, of course, goes out of his minimind with excitement.

What is Dad thinking?

Mama is a monument of indignation.

Thomas is six years old! He can't even tie his own shoes! When Dad replies he learned to shoot at that age, like most island boys do, and did she ever consider she babies that boy too much, Mama brings up her Cleveland cousin who got shot, a terrible story that always makes her cry.

It's downhill from there.

Flor is upstairs on the landing, guarding the phone, waiting for Sylvie to call. Thomas crouches beside her, shooting his finger between the spindles of the banister. Cecilia? Maybe she's in her room. Maybe she's gone. Basically these days it's the same thing.

Mama says, "You always . . ." and "You never . . ." Dad dwindles. Sunlight tumbles through the landing window and tries to tickle Flor's feet. The day is pretending nothing's wrong. *Look at me,* it says. *I'm all about sunshine and happiness!*

Not here. Not in this house.

"Bang!" Thomas whispers. "Bang!" But after firing off a few more rounds, he lets his arm fall to his side.

"Never mind." He leans over the banister. "I don't

want to go anyway. It's not worth it."

A pause. Both parents look up, and for about three seconds they both look sorry. Even a little ashamed. For three seconds, they could be TV parents, who realize the error of their ways, and order in pizza, and start holding family meetings where every opinion matters, and here comes the happy ending, lifting you on its wings.

For three seconds.

"Go out and play, you two," Dad says then. "We'll settle this. It's not your business."

Even Thomas recognizes this for the insult it is. He balls his fists. He puffs his cheeks. As if they're babies! As if they don't notice, or will forget, the things that get said around here. As if how their parents hurt each other is *not their business*?

Flor grips the phone, which refuses to ring. If only Sylvie still lived here, Flor could escape to her house now. If only Cecilia hadn't disowned them, Flor wouldn't be on her own now. Lonesomeness chokes her insides like a garden full of weeds.

"Go on!" Mama shoos her hands. "You heard your father."

"No!" Flor's had it. She shoos her hands back. "It

is our business. We live here. This is our house as much as yours!"

"What did I tell you about flipping that lip?" Mama's hands go to her hips.

"Don't make her more madder," Thomas begs.

Too late now. Flor's had enough. Enough! She's got no one to turn to except her own self, and if she doesn't say what's inside her, something bad will happen. She will wither. Shrivel. Maybe even disappear, wink right out, that's how it feels. Mama shakes a finger. Flor shakes hers back.

"If we fight we get punished!" The words tear out of her. "You should too!"

Like Flor broke some curse, Cecilia's door blasts open. She was in there after all!

"Flor's right!" Cecilia's eyes and mouth are big. Huge. "We're sick of you fighting! What's wrong with you? Why don't you stop? Do you need professional help? Are you psychotic?"

Dad has started climbing the steps, but he freezes. Cecilia? Cecilia flipping the lip?

"Cele's right!" cries Flor. "This is all messed up! It's not how a family's supposed to be."

"Everybody's yelling." Thomas puts his hands over his ears. "Please stop yelling, please."

"You don't just hurt each other! You hurt us too!" Cecilia leans over the railing, pointing, accusing. "Don't you see that? Or don't you even care?"

Her sister taking her side turns Flor bold and crazy.

"You're so selfish!" she shouts. "You should be ashamed!"

"That's enough!" yells Dad. "Enough out of you both!"

"I hate this!" cries Cecilia. "Hate it! You make me want to run away!"

Run away!

That's too much for Thomas. He starts to wail. Which makes Flor feel terrible, but there's no stopping her big mouth.

"No! If they hate each other so much, one of *them* should go! Just get it over with!"

Thomas wails louder. Even Cecilia looks shocked.

Flor's clattering down the stairs, stumbling at the bottom, tripping headlong toward the door, and neither parent tries to stop her. Good! Because they can't. She spoke the truth and she feels terrific. Terrific! She grabs her backpack from the hook and bangs out into the too-bright, too-cheerful sunshine. It's so bright, for a moment she's blind.

That's when she realizes she's still holding the cordless phone. Which hasn't rung, like it's frightened too. No way is Flor going back into that house. She shoves the phone into her backpack, grabs her bike, and jumps on.

"Flor! Stay! Stay!" Her brother's in the yard. His thin voice chases her down the road.

chapter nine

Flor digs her toes into the rim of the old quarry.
Her heart's a circus, with trapezes and tightropes
and people shooting out of cannons but no nets—
someone forgot the nets. She can still hear Thomas
begging her to stay. And Cecilia threatening to run
away. Loudest of all is her own voice, saying "One of
them should *go, go, go*. . . ."

Usually, riding her bike till she nearly has a heart
attack calms her down, but not today. Today everything's different. Even Moonpenny Quarry. It quivers
in the sunshine, rays of light bouncing off the rocks

or getting sucked into the dense, scrubby junipers. The quarry is supposed to be peaceful, but this afternoon it buzzes with secret energy, crackles with a life all its own. Flor hesitates, but where else can she go?

The loose dirt under her feet gives way, and she grabs the trunk of a tree to keep from falling. The tree's roots grip the rim for dear life. Nearby, a crumpled, dried-up skin. Shucked off by a snake, that slid away all sleek and new.

Flor's not sorry for what she said. Not. She presses a hand to her heart, feels it beat beat beat. Not. Not. Not.

Maybe she will be. But not yet.

Hate. She shouldn't have used that word.

Cecilia said it too.

A familiar bark and squeak turn her around.

Old Violet Tinkiss and her two-legged dog trundle down the road. Violet's hair is a crazy thundercloud. She barely glances at Flor, but little Minnie, strapped into the doggie-wheelchair contraption Violet built her, smiles her pink-gummed smile. Her useless rear legs flap like extra tails. Digging into her backpack, Flor pulls out one of the dog treats she carries just in case she meets up with Minnie.

"Hey, sweet girl." She fondles the dog's long, silky ears. "How you doing, Violet?"

Violet grunts. Her being here is an undeniable sign that summer's over. During tourist season, Violet lies low, sticking to her dilapidated fishing shack or camping at the abandoned rescue station out on the neck. She mutters and curses, maybe at the lake, where her husband's ship wrecked fifty years ago, or at the heartless summer person who hit Minnie and left her lying in a ditch, or maybe at the cruel universe in general. Dad's the only human being she tolerates.

But now she'll be out and about, like some animal that hibernates in reverse. It's funny how the island's crazy person makes Flor feel more normal. She tells herself it'll be all right. Mama will punish her, but eventually her parents will make up, just like always. Thomas will go back to being annoying. And Cecilia. Clearly she's had a change of heart. She won't freeze Flor out, not after this.

It'll be a while, though, till things calm down back there. She watches Violet and Minnie wheel away, then peg-legs her way down the side of the quarry. Loose stones skitter. A rabbit shoots out from one thorny bush and hides behind another. Flor picks her way around the tumbled rocks to where the cattails whisper among themselves. Parting them, she slips through, steps out onto the edge of the swimming hole.

Stretching out, chin on her fist, she peers into the icy water. The bodies of those drowned lovers still lie down there. On a ledge, Joe Hawkins says. He claims he saw their bones, bleached out and picked clean. The skeletons still have their gnarly arms around each other, locked in eternal frozen embrace. Minnows swim in and out of their eye sockets.

Joe Hawkins! Only someone certified brainless would believe him!

The water ripples, though no one threw a stone. The shadow of a cloud whisks across the water and brings with it Flor's bad dream. On a ledge, in the dark.

Maybe things won't be all right.

Flor gives herself a shake. Stop that right now. She sits up and opens her backpack. The phone. Of course it won't work out here. Still she presses TALK and holds it to her ear.

"Hello? Hello, Sylvie? Why didn't you call? I really, really need to talk to you."

Thank goodness no one can see her.

"You could put shaving cream on your lips and say a rabid squirrel bit you. You could fake the symptoms of malaria. Chills and fever."

No reply. Flor puts the phone away and stretches out on the refrigerator rock. She opens her library book. Moonpenny Public Library is in the basement of the school, and the comforting smell of underground wafts out. After a while, she rests her cheek against the page. A breeze strokes the back of her neck. Quarry quiet. It's so deep down.

Pock!

Her eyes fly open. Drool glues her cheek to the page. She must have drifted off.

Pock, pock!

Sitting up, rubbing her eyes, Flor knows what that sound is. Dad at the VFW, practicing his shooting. Every single Saturday, come hell or high water.

The sun's slipped a few notches, and when she stands up, her shadow wears stilts. She has to go home right now. Making Mama madder is the last thing anyone needs. She wipes the drool off her book, shoves it into her pack. She picks up the phone.

"I'm on my way home, Sylvie. In case you've been trying and trying to reach me and are worried where I am. I mean, really frantically worried, since you are my best friend and care about me above all other living creatures."

Her foot has fallen asleep. It's encased in a block of cement. Dragging it behind her, she stumbles through the cattails, out into the open quarry, and directly into a girl wearing work boots with red laces and a sweatshirt big enough for three more of her to fit inside. Jumping back, the girl swings up a phone and snaps her photo.

"What are you doing? You took my picture?" Flor shoves her dead phone into her backpack. Her face burns. "You're spying again!"

"No! Not this time."

"See! You admit it!"

"Spying, observing, go on—waste time splitting hairs."

Pock pock pock! Three more shots dent the air.

The girl turtles inside her XXL sweatshirt. Her eyes flick from side to side.

"My father's taking target practice," Flor says. "It's just practice bullets, not real."

"Your father's the police officer." The sweatshirt muffles her voice. "He should get a new patrol car. His spews out way too much exhaust. It's very bad for the environment."

Her eyes are green and her hair is fizzy, like ginger ale. Flor's waked-up foot is getting stabbed by fiery pins and needles.

"He can't help what it spews out. That car's the best this island can afford."

"That's too bad." She pulls the sweatshirt down. "I'm doing reconnaissance for *my* father, who, as you probably know, is a geologist with a special interest in *Phacops rana*."

"No. I did not know that." How strange is this girl? Very. And what is with that giant sweatshirt?

The girl holds up her phone, which has a camouflage cover. She's into being invisible, it seems. There's something odd about how she palms and swipes the screen, but before Flor can think what, she's being forced to look at photos.

"Rocks," says Flor.

"Observe more closely."

"Oh. Fossils."

Once, forever ago, all of Moonpenny lay underwater. A great inland sea covered everything. If Flor had been alive back then—well, she'd have been a prehistoric shark or bit of coral, since no humans existed yet. Island limestone is perfect for the formation of fossils. Every island kid has a few in a shoe box.

The girl pauses at a photo of a miniature cone, its tail curled in on itself.

"Popular name, horn coral. Scientific name, *Sterolasma rectum*." Swipe. "Brachiopod." Swipe. "Rhipidomella."

She's showing off, naming everything, like she owns the place, when Flor—Flor!—is the one who lives here. The girl, whose own name remains a mystery, slides her eyes sideways, making sure Flor's paying attention.

"And here we have *Homo sapiens*."

A blur of a girl, with skin the color of cauliflower

and a useless phone pressed to her ear. You could put a whole apple in her mouth, that's how wide open it is. Flor always looks bad in photos, but this wins the gold.

Before she can squawk, the girl hits DELETE and the picture disappears.

"Well," says Flor. "Thank you for that."

Her phone really rings.

"Hello, Father. . . . A few interesting finds. I've noted the coordinates. . . . Fifteen minutes. No more, I promise." She drops the phone into the messenger bag slung across her chest, then stands there doing an imitation of someone who hates to go.

"By the way, my name is Jasper Fife. Jasper is a form of crystalline quartz, and it's often green." She points at her eyes. "You're Flora."

"Flor. No ah."

Overhead, a flock of ducks wings by. One brings up the rear, flapping and quacking. *Wait up, guys! Wait for me!* Then things get quiet again. Dad's long done shooting. He'll be at the police station now, carefully cleaning his gun before locking it back up. Afterward, he's supposed to stop at Two Sisters and get the popcorn for their Saturday-night treat. Later, they're all supposed to squish together on the couch and watch a movie. Flor tries her best to imagine all this happening.

"Is something the matter?" Jasper is regarding her like a specimen in need of a scientific name.

"What?"

"You look pale and sickly."

"I always look like this."

Jasper starts climbing up the side of the quarry. She's clumsy, slipping and sliding and clawing at saplings with one hand. It's exhausting to watch. And a huge surprise when, finally at the top, she turns and calls down, "Do you want to meet my father?"

"What?"

"He'll show you his fossils." Jasper pauses. "Feel free to decline."

Flor has to go home. She absolutely does.

"Okay," she says. "Just for a minute."

chapter ten

Every spring and fall, Moonpenny Island becomes a bird motel. Migrating across the lake, the birds stop here to rest and eat, and on weekends the Red Robin Inn fills up with people wearing fancy binoculars around their necks. Bird brains, the islanders call them. A couple of birders perch in rockers on the inn's front porch and cock their birdlike heads at Flor and Jasper as they go inside.

In the lobby, a small man with a big white beard and boots that are a replica of Jasper's greets them.

"Here she is! My little animalcule!"

A bony Santa. If Santa dressed in hiking boots and a tool belt. A dirt comet streaks across his cheek. Licking her finger, Jasper rubs it clean. She's as tall as he is.

"And who's this?" His dark eyes twinkle, which is something Flor thought only happened in books. He grabs her hand and pumps it. "I'm Dr. Fife."

"Father, this is Flor."

"And are you native to the island, Miss Flora and Fauna?"

"Umm, I guess so."

He shakes Flor's hand for a century or two. She gets the distinct feeling that Jasper doesn't bring people home every day.

"You look hungry!" he says. "Follow me!"

The wooden steps creak. Dr. Fife's socks droop around his ankles. Up, up, up they climb, to the top floor, where they step into a big room with a slanted roof and a tall window at either end. Beneath each window there's an unmade bed. In the room's center, chaos. A couch swamped with dirty dishes, and a long table buried under maps, rocks, rolls of strapping tape, a laptop, rocks, notebooks, a camera, wadded-up paper towels, rocks, spray bottles, tools, knives, and labeled ziplock bags. And rocks.

"Give us a moment," says Dr. Fife.

He sweeps aside mugs and forks to make room on the couch. Meanwhile, Jasper pulls a ham out of the mini refrigerator and starts hacking it up. The sight sets Flor's mouth watering. She didn't eat lunch, and she loves ham.

Ham, it turns out, is it. Ham and more ham, with a couple of slices of bread thrown in for a second food group. It's like camping out indoors. Dr. Fife wolfs down a few chunks, then goes to the worktable. He chooses a rock and a teensy pick that reminds Flor of the one the dental hygienist uses to clean her teeth. Pick pick pick, till he switches to a knife, and then whittle whittle whittle. His movements are small and quick. The couch, the floor—everything's covered with fine, stony dust. Something tells Flor there's no mother in this picture.

Dr. Fife shows her the rock. Tiny tunnels run through it every which way.

"Trilobites," he tells her. "Expert burrowers! Humble heroes of the remarkable Cambrian period."

Flor knows about trilobites. They resembled a cross between a beetle and a miniature armored tank and scuttled around in the mud at the bottom of ye olde prehistoric sea. When they took an all-school field trip to the Cleveland Museum of Natural History, Mrs. Defoe demanded they admire the dusty case of trilobites, the state fossil. Yawn! Snooze! The real stars of the show were the dinosaurs and the prehistoric sharks with teeth the size of bananas.

"So the trilobite's your specialty?" she asks, trying to be polite, thinking, You can't map the ways of the heart.

It's like Jasper's father got plugged into a socket. She almost hears him start to hum. Yes, it is his specialty, and specifically the trilobite eye. Does she know the trilobite was among the very first creatures to develop eyes?

Flor shakes her head. Wait. Does this mean there were once creatures *without eyes*? A shudder goes through her.

"The wily *Acaste*, the lumbering *Paradoxides*, and the ubiquitous *Phacops*—they all evolved to have high-quality vision! And let's not forget those entrepreneurs who developed eyes mounted on stalks. That enabled them to immerse themselves in sediment but still keep an eye out for predators." Dr. Fife claps his hands. "*Literally* keep an eye out!"

"But I thought all creatures had eyes," Flor says. "I mean, I thought eyes were part of being a creature."

"Sight had to evolve, just like everything else," says Dr. Fife.

"Do you know what *evolve* means?" Jasper's deep voice makes everything she says sound like a lesson.

"Of course I do! Like, we evolved from apes."

"Wrong." Jasper shakes her head. "A common misconception."

"Yes, well. Our Flora and Fauna has the general idea." Dr. Fife looks pained, either at Flor's ignorance or Jasper's rudeness or maybe both. "I bet she knows who Charles Darwin was."

"She does," says Flor. "I mean, I do." Charles Darwin? She's heard that name somewhere.

"The earliest eyes were simple optic nerves coated with pigment. Very primitive, but they gave those creatures a definite advantage." Dr. Fife tugs his beard. "They could find food more easily and avoid their predators. Over time, those eyes changed and developed, and the most useful variations were passed on to the offspring. Again and again and yes, again. And so the eye evolved into one of the most complex organs imaginable." His own deep-set eyes shine. "Darwin's theory, as you know!"

Flor nods. Sure! Got it! Meanwhile, a voice inside her squawks, *What!* What if eyes didn't develop? What if people had to fumble their way around using their noses or ears or—gross—tongues instead?

"Trilobites were sturdy little fellows. They very thoughtfully left behind an abundant fossil record. By studying it, we can trace how they evolved to have sight as crystal clear as any animal living today." He picks up his drill. "We've already found some prime specimens here, Flor. Your island is a tectonic treasure trove!" Switching on the drill, he gets back to work.

"Well, if trilobites were that amazing, how come they went extinct?" Flor asks. Bent over his work, Dr. Fife doesn't hear, so she turns to Jasper, who's now playing a game on her phone. "How come . . ."

"Asteroids. Changes in climate," says Jasper, not looking up. "And they were invertebrates. They wore their protection on the outside and kept the soft parts inside, the opposite of us."

"But wouldn't that keep them safer?"

"Only one problem. They grew. Their shells became prisons they had to cast off. Till they grew a new one, they had to go around naked. They were easy targets for predators. Eventually the predators wiped them all out."

"That's so sad. That's pitiful."

"Many of their predators went extinct too. Due to other, larger predators."

"I hate predators."

Jasper looks up. Her eyes are so green. "Me too."

Dr. Fife keeps working. Flor wonders if this is how things go here every night, Jasper and her father, the two of them together but alone.

"You don't go to school?"

"I did for a while. Speaking of predators." A shadow crosses Jasper's face, and she looks back down. "It was not a successful experiment. So now I'm homeschooled."

"Isn't that kind of, you know. Lonely?"

"I've observed you in the school yard. You look

like the last remaining member of a species on the verge of extinction."

Flor stiffens. "My best friend moved away."

Jasper's thumb pauses midair. "You'll make a new friend."

"Impossible."

Jasper's thumb hovers. "Then you're doomed to friendlessness."

"I didn't say that." But did she?

Jasper's thumb descends, too late. Boom. Game over. She makes a disgusted sound.

"How come you only play with one hand?"

Jasper's green eyes get darker, like when you walk deeper into a forest. She's struggling to decide something, Flor can tell.

"I only have one," she finally says.

"Only one game?" Flor's confused.

"Hand."

Jasper hesitates another moment, then makes up her mind. With a last look at Flor, she's rolling up one of her mile-long sleeves. Rolling and rolling, but nothing appears.

Until it does. A dented pink nub. A few inches

104

up, there's a normal elbow and the rest of an arm. But that nub. Flor stares. She can't help it. It's like a sightless creature.

"It's a birth defect." Jasper could be the voice on an educational film. "It's called amniotic band syndrome, or ABS. It happened in utero—in other words, before I was born."

"Oh. Okay." Flor's voice squeaks. She looks away. "I didn't notice. I mean . . ."

"I know. You're not very observant." Jasper rolls her sleeve back down. "Now you really are pale."

Across the room, Dr. Fife has missed the whole thing. He might have forgotten she's even here. It's him and the trilobites. The room's lonesome feeling suddenly becomes so strong, all Flor wants is to go home. Even if Mama and Dad raise the roof again tonight, home is where she wants to be.

"I have to go," she squeaks.

She takes her plate to the sink, which is full of rocks, and swings her backpack over her shoulder.

"Thanks for everything." she says, and starts for the door.

"Going already?" Dr. Fife looks up, distressed.

"Would you like more ham? Or some lemonade?" He glances around the room, like maybe there's something else he can offer to make her stay and be Jasper's friend. But all he's got are rocks.

"She has to go!" says Jasper. Probably she wishes she hadn't shown Flor her arm. Probably she's wishing this pale, squeamish, unobservant girl would leave as quickly as possible. She walks Flor to the room's door, then shuts it firmly behind her.

The inn's porch is empty. The birders, who get up before dawn, must have gone to bed. Bats swoop in and out of the yellow light at the end of the walkway, and high in a tree, a ghost shrieks.

Stop it right now, Flor tells herself. That is a screech owl and you know it!

She hates the dark. She'll have to ride as fast as she can.

No! She smacks her forehead. Her bike! It's still back at the quarry, where she left it when she walked here with Jasper.

Flor doesn't know what to do. She can't go all the way back to the quarry now. She can walk home, but it will take forever, and the dark is very dark.

Streetlights are few and far between on Moonpenny, and where is the moon? No moon. She could go back in and ask to borrow the phone, but her parents will already be angry at her, and having to pick her up will make things worse. Why didn't Dr. Fife offer to drive her? A normal parent would never let a kid leave by herself after dark.

That pink nub where an arm and hand should be. Flor rubs her own two arms, creepy with goose bumps.

Walk. She'll just walk, that's all. She's way too old to be this afraid of the dark.

Within seconds, the friendly yellow light of the inn is history. Some closed-up cottages and then it's nothing except a wall of trees on either side. If she cranes her neck, she can spy a few cold white pinpricks. She could be a trilobite, crawling in the murky mud at the base of the inland sea. She could be a sack of bones lying at the bottom of the swim hole. If it had a bottom.

Sylvie tried to help her get over her fear of the dark. Flor strains to remember some of the things she'd say. "Night is when the world does stuff it doesn't want people to see. Trees and flowers grow, and beautiful moths come out of their cocoons. Little baby fawns get born. Nighttime is magic time, Flor!"

Sylvie would die before she'd let Flor walk home alone in the dark.

All that ham made Flor so thirsty, she can hardly swallow. That owl screeches. Predators! She hates predators. One foot in front of the other. Her backpack bumps between her shoulder blades. Her heart bumps in her chest. In the distance she can hear the lake. *Grow up,* it scolds. *You silly scaredy-cat girl.*

Above her, the air goes electric, then hollow. Something swift and silent scoops it clean, and Flor flings her hands over her head. The grass beside the road parts, and she can sense the owl, his spread wings, his sharp beak and steely talons. Eeek! A pitiful scream rises from the grass. It cuts off abruptly, and the night closes back up, once more deathly quiet, except for that small whimpering sound.

Which is her. Flor herself. She leans against a tree, scooped out and hollow herself. Home is still so far away. Her legs are so heavy.

"I am all alone," she whispers.

Headlights sweep the road. If only they stop! If only they offer her a ride!

And they do! The headlights pick her out, blinding her. It's not till the truck stops and the passenger door swings open that she can tell who it is, and by then it's too late.

"You!" says Peregrine Pinch the Fourth. "Where the freak have you been?"

chapter eleven

His blond hair shines in the dark. It hangs over his eyes so he has to keep pushing it away, but of course it just falls right back. Even Sylvie's beautiful hair isn't that bright and shiny, like a star burning itself up.

In the passenger seat, Flor puts as much distance as she can between her and him. She surreptitiously sniffs the air, trying to detect the smell of beer or drugs, though who knows what drugs smell like. Perry drives with one hand, practically one finger, which is precisely how someone who nearly killed himself in an accident should not drive.

He smells like soap, that's all. He's tried to wash away all the badness. He can't fool her, though.

"What are you doing out all alone?" he demands. Like he has any right.

"Visiting a friend."

"A friend?" He turns to look at her. "You made a new friend?"

Flor stares straight ahead. "Would that be so amazing?" she wants to say. "Keep your eyes on the road," she should say. "Shape up and do not even think about running away," she promised Sylvie to say.

But her tongue is in a knot. From the corner of her eye, she watches him push his blond, blazing hair out of his eyes. Last year, Lauren Long tried to bribe Sylvie to steal one of his T-shirts for her. His hair flops back in his eyes.

"You miss my sister, don't you."

Not a question, she notices. Flor hugs her backpack tight against her chest. Being alone with Perry feels aloner than with other people. He's driving way too fast.

"But it's good she went away," he says next.

"What?" Her tongue unknots.

"It's good for her."

"No. No, I don't think so. It'd be way better if she stayed here. You and I both need her."

She didn't mean to say that! Lumping herself together with him. Dark trees rush by the windows.

"You're right," he says. "But what I said is, it's good for *her*."

What is this? Is he trying to make Flor feel bad? Like he knows what Sylvie needs. Like he even cares!

"We'll see about that," she says. Thomas's stupid phrase! What is wrong with her mouth? It's done nothing but cause trouble and blurt stupid things all day long. The truck slows down. Moments ago it seemed like she'd never get home, but look, here they are already, the gravel driveway crunching beneath the truck's tires.

Perry leans to open her door, and she breathes in the smell of soap and something else she has no name for. A spark races upward and sets her cheeks on fire. She jumps out.

"Thanks for the ride." Mama will have a falling-down fit over her taking a ride with him. Mama!

She's already in so much trouble with Mama. She'll have to lie about how she got here.

"Don't let me catch you out alone after dark again."

Like he's her big brother! Flor's cheeks burn. Long long ago, he actually played with her and Sylvie. He'd ride them piggyback, buy them candy at Two Sisters. Sometimes at night, while they watched TV, he even let them play beauty parlor on him. They'd twist his beautiful hair into tiny braids and clip it with barrettes. Flor still remembers how soft his hair felt. Soft as milkweed down.

Does Perry still remember that? A sudden smile lights up his face, like something buried rising into the light. A rare pleated shell, poking through the surface of a rock.

This is why Sylvie loves him so. For a heartbeat, Flor loves him too.

What!

"You better call your sister right away," she says, her knees wobbling. "Like yesterday, you hear me? She really wants to talk to you."

"Got it, chief." He nods, then juts his chin toward

the house. "Hey. Sorry about what's going on."

The door slams, the pickup roars away. Why does he have to drive so fast?

Going on?

Flor streaks across the grass. The second she steps inside, her whole family boils up around her, hugging and scolding.

Wait. Not her whole family.

"Where's Mama?"

"Did someone drop you off?" Cecilia parts the curtain. "Did I hear a pickup?"

"I drove all over creation looking for you," says Dad. "I didn't even get to clean my gun."

"We can't find the phone." Cecilia turns from the window. "I used my cell to call everyone, but nobody had seen you."

"Everything happened so fast," says Dad.

"What happened? Where's Mama?"

"You ran away." Thomas is sucking Snowball's ear. "I said don't go, but you still did."

"I'd *never* run away! I . . ."

"All of a sudden, it's an emergency," says Dad. He runs his hand through his hair. "Just like that, everything's changed."

"Somebody better tell me where Mama is!" Flor shouts. "Right now!"

Quiet.

"Lita's sick." Dad puts his big arm around her. His voice turns gentle. "That cold of hers got worse and the aunts finally made her go to the doctor. It's bronchitis. She'll be all right, don't worry."

"But where's Mama?"

Dad's arm slides off her shoulder. He runs his hand across his head again. His hair stands up, petrified.

"She'd be beside herself staying here, Flor. She needs to be with her family."

The three of them stand around him in a little circle, like they're about to join hands and play a game. We're her family. Flor can't be the only one thinking that.

"It's just for a little while," Dad goes on. "A few days, tops. We'll all pitch in. It'll be an adventure!" He picks up Thomas and spins him around. "You ready for an adventure, old buddy?"

One of you should go. Should go. Go.

Cecilia pries Flor's backpack out of her arms.

"She really wanted to say good-bye to you. She said to tell you she'll call tomorrow."

Without the backpack, Flor's arms feel unbearably empty. They flop around. Cecilia tucks Flor's hair behind her ear. She smells like soap and something else.

"Hey," Cecilia says. "You know what? It might be good she went."

What Perry just said about Sylvie! Something inside Flor gives a hard, painful twist.

"Maybe," Flor says. "If Lita gets better and she comes right back."

But Cecilia means something else. She hangs the backpack on a hook and turns to Flor. Her eye makeup is smudged. It makes her look even older and more beautiful, like in a movie when the star just gets out of bed.

"You were right. What you said this afternoon? Maybe Mama going—it's the right thing. Maybe it's the only way things can change around here."

"I never said that. What's that supposed to mean?"

But Cecilia's black hair swings across her face as she turns away. So much for *her* changing. So much for her behaving like she and Flor actually have something in common besides the same name and parents

116

and living in the same house!

Later, Flor's in bed, not falling asleep, when she sits up so quickly she goes light-headed. When Perry told her "sorry about what's going on"? He must have already known Mama was gone. Word travels fast on Moonpenny, but still. It's wrong that he knew before she did. He's the last person she'd pick to know her business, the last person she wants feeling sorry for her.

Getting out of bed, she picks up Sylvie's fossil. Jasper Fife would spout its scientific name, but a name is not the point, not with this fossil. Can you make *four* wishes on the very same fossil? Flor closes her eyes. Hopes so. Hopes.

chapter twelve

Without Mama's voice, the church choir sounds pathetic. It's all Flor can do not to cover her ears. The islanders spread themselves around the mostly empty church, a family in this pew, an old lady in that one, the way Thomas breaks a cookie into pieces to convince himself he's got more than he really does.

Flor prays for Lita. Prays for Mama.

Monday she stands in the school yard shivering. Mama would've checked the weather and made her wear her jacket, but instead she's just got this flimsy sweater. Thomas wears shorts and two different-colored socks. He sits on a swing, pretending to smoke a crayon. Cecilia's with the other high schoolers, but not really. How far away is her mind? Light-years, Flor can tell.

Still 11:16. Flor quit paying attention to that clock long ago, but today it makes her depressed. Time can't stop—things are too messed up. Time needs to get going, move along and make things better. But the stubborn hands refuse to move. They haven't moved in so long, some bird made her nest behind the hour hand.

There's an expression "No man is an island," but apparently eleven-year-old girls can be. Being a one-hundred-percent isolated person leaves you time to notice things you missed before, when your faithful friend was forever at your side. Flor sees Lauren Long laugh, then look pointedly at Cecilia. Sees her sister's laugh come a beat too late. Sees Lauren's snarky look bounce to the other two girls. Sees Cecilia flush and press her lips together.

She sees a distant flock of birds splatter the sky like dark paint. Sees Mary Long stop complaining about her allergies long enough to scream "Don't!" when Larry Walnut walks by, minding his own business. Sees Larry stagger and look amazed. How can he possibly not know Mary is cuckoo for him? How can she possibly be cuckoo for him? Are they both blind?

Blindness was once a natural state. Dr. Fife says the first eye was little more than an optic nerve. Whatever that is. Eyes had to develop. Can some people's eyes still be a more primitive variety? Can eyes still be evolving? Will future humans be able to see stuff we can't? Like the insides of things. The hidden, secret parts?

Jasper would know. Flor peers across the road, where the lilac bush is uninhabited, unless you count the sparrows hopping among the dried-up flowers. FREE FILL DIRT says the cemetery sign. Flor's read it a hundred times, but never thought what it actually means, till now. Her knees go weak. Her knee muscles seem to be deteriorating. She's cold all through. Recess must be going on longer than usual, though how can she be sure, considering the stupid clock says 11:16 no matter what?

"Look what I found."

Flor turns around. Jocelyn Hawkins extends a hand.

"A fossil," says Flor, and can't help but add, "It's horn coral."

"No. It's a shark tooth."

"I don't think so."

"I found it. It's what I say." Casting a withering look, Jocelyn stomps over to her brother Joe, who's using a small wrench to tighten bolts on the wooden climber. "Isn't this a shark tooth?"

A quick glance. "Nope. Horn coral."

"Oh." She throws it in the dirt like a piece of trash, then scrambles up the climber. The red-and-blue lights work on only one of her hand-me-down sneakers.

"She wouldn't believe me," says Flor.

Joe shrugs. "Prehistoric roadkill is prehistoric roadkill."

He tightens another bolt. His curls are wild and thick, and this must be where the word *ringlet* comes from—slide your finger through one, and you'd be wearing a shiny band. Suddenly Flor's cheeks are the only part of her that's warm.

"What are you doing that for?" she blurts. "It's your father's job."

Come to think of it, she's often seen him before or after school, hauling a ladder or carrying a mop and bucket. How much of his father's work does he do? How much does he cover up for his dad? And why hasn't she ever noticed before? To her surprise, Joe looks nervous, like he got caught at something. He changes the subject.

"Want to know a secret about Defoe?" he says.

"Sure."

"She konks out at lunchtime."

"She does?"

"She puts her head down on her desk and snores her big blockhead off. My dad's seen her."

"She's pretty old."

"Try prehistoric."

"Archaic."

"Antique."

"Ancient."

"Antediluvian."

"You win," says Flor, and Joe laughs.

"You're nicer without that Sylvie Pinch around," he says.

"What?"

"Okay, maybe you were always nice. But it was hard to tell, since you two were like a secret society or something."

"Help! I'm stuck!" shrieks Jocelyn, and even though she's just being a drama queen, he scrambles up to rescue her. Jocelyn throws her arms around his neck and presses her little cheek to his. For a girl in a Toledo Mud Hens sweatshirt, she manages to be very girly. Joe sets her on her feet, pats her head, and throws a rock at the clock tower. Jocelyn sticks her tongue out at Flor.

Later, Flor ponders whether that's dried drool or milk on the corner of her teacher's mouth. Mrs. Defoe is always on Mr. Hawkins's case, directing him to burned-out lightbulbs or leaky faucets he's neglected. Poor Mr. Hawkins. Out of school but still her minion. Maybe he made up the nap story, to get back at her. It's not like adults are above bad behavior.

Her mind slides toward Mama. Who will not

be there when they get home, standing in her usual place by the sink, chopping peppers and onions so fast the knife's a blur. A small, invisible blade stabs Flor's heart. On the phone last night, Mama told Flor to help Dad, mind Cecilia, and make sure Thomas changes his socks. She sounded stern but also strangely cheerful. Flor could hear the clatter of pots and pans in the background, Titi Aurora or Carmen or Gloria scolding and laughing. She strained to hear *I miss you* in Mama's voice.

"Flor." Mrs. Defoe is calling her up for sixth-grade language arts. On her desk lies a copy of *Anne of Avonlea*, by L. M. Montgomery. Flor has already read it. She loves the heroine, Anne Shirley, with her red hair, her pale (pale!) skin, her seven freckles, and her wild, free heart. It's old-fashioned, the kind of book that makes Sylvie's eyes roll up inside her head, but Flor found it wonderful.

Dried drool, definitely. Flor cuts her eyes at Joe, who clunks his head onto his desk and makes a soft but unmistakable snoring sound.

"I've assigned this book to every sixth grader for forty-four years, and do you know why?" Mrs.

Defoe's voice is hushed. Like she's about to reveal a deep, meaningful secret. Flor tries not to look at the dried drool. She feels a drop of dread. Mrs. Defoe draws a breath.

"I first discovered it when I was your age. This book is the reason I became a teacher. Anne Shirley inspired me."

This is sad. Tragic, actually. Anne Shirley's eyes are always shining, her cheeks flushing, her hair streaming behind her in a torrent of brightness. Drab old Mrs. Defoe and lively, fun-loving Anne Shirley have nothing whatsoever in common. Well, they both live on islands, but there it ends.

Mrs. Defoe goes on and on about Anne and the torch of knowledge. Flor tries to hide her disbelief. Feeling sorry for an adult is so confusing.

"I liked it," she says.

"You've already read it?" Mrs. Defoe looks offended. "Well, Flor O'Dell, you are about to reread it." She hands Flor a sheet of paper obviously typed on a typewriter, that's how old it is. How antediluvian. "Your six-hundred-word book report is due in two weeks. Follow this format without deviation."

Joe unleashes a volcanic snort.

"Joseph Hawkins Junior to my desk," Mrs. Defoe barks. "Once again!"

"It's true," Flor whispers to him, pointing at the corner of her mouth, and he smiles.

Mrs. Defoe tells Joe that despite his continuing efforts to appear ignorant and intractable, she's not giving up on him. Joe shrugs. He's a shrugger, all right. *Who cares?* is his message. It's a useful one, considering what people think of the Hawkins family. Mrs. Defoe invites him to take a seat out in the hall.

But as he saunters out, Flor wonders if it's all an act. A shell to ward off predators, like the trilobites had. Except they outgrew theirs, and had to cast them off, and wander around naked for a while.

Joe Hawkins and naked? Who let those words into her head at the same time? Flor slides down in her seat. Thank goodness only Sylvie can read her mind.

After school she and Thomas ride home together. His legs are so short and pudgy, she could easily leave him in the dust, but not today. Something about the trusting way Jocelyn looked at Joe makes her want to be nice, the kind of big sister you can count on.

Unlike her own.

Thomas begs to stop at the old quarry, where he's forbidden to go alone, and even though Flor needs to pee, she says, in her new, kindly-sister voice, "Okay, just for a second."

Standing on the rim, they see Dr. Fife and Jasper down there, hard at work. He's pounding small stakes into the ground. She's measuring, handing him tools.

"What are they doing?" Thomas asks.

"Excavating. They dig up stuff."

That's all Thomas needs to hear. Flor grabs him as he starts to butt slide down.

"Let go!" Another of his talents: the set-your-teeth-on-edge whine. "You're hurting me! Let me go!"

Jasper looks up and waves. The half-empty sleeve of her big shirt flaps around.

"You're spying on us!" she calls, shading her eyes.

Thomas squirms, but Flor hangs on. Is Jasper accusing or teasing? Flor can't be sure, and besides, she still feels bad about the other night at the inn. She's pretty sure Jasper doesn't go around revealing her ABS arm to everybody—why else would she hide it inside those crazy-big clothes? For some reason, she trusted Flor. Who acted like she couldn't wait to get away. Which she couldn't. Only now she feels bad. Only not bad enough to go down there and be nice.

"I have to pee," she whispers to Thomas.

"Go in the bushes!"

"Maybe you're an animal, but I'm not."

"My sister has to pee," he hollers as she drags him away.

chapter thirteen

Even though Mama left in such a sudden way, she somehow managed to stock the freezer full. Container after container of spaghetti sauce, chili, stew, and several trays of frijoles. At dinner that night, Cecilia picks at a salad. She says she's turned vegetarian. Mama would fall into a dead faint, but Dad just drums his fingers on the table. It's not like he's got a big appetite, either. Thomas's hands are sparkling clean as far as his wrists, where the dirt takes over. He picks at a scab on his elbow till Flor yells is he trying to make her barf?

Lita's doctor claims the antibiotics should be working by now, but Mama says when Lita coughs it's like a wolf gets her in its jaws and shakes her head to toe. That makes Flor feels terrible. How can she be thinking only of herself, when her grandmother's so sick? Mama tells her to mind her temper and to be sure Thomas wears clean underwear. She says Cecilia is taking her place, and Flor has to do everything her big sister tells her, does Flor understand? Everything. Flor starts to protest that Cecilia doesn't care if they live or die but Mama just cuts her off. Repeat, Cecilia is the substitute mother, and now please put her on the phone. After Cecilia comes Thomas, who doesn't say a word, just nods and breathes through his mouth. Finally Dad takes the phone. He inhales like he's preparing to run ten miles, or appear before the Supreme Court.

"Hello, Beatriz." Her whole name, like she's a stranger and they just met. He and the phone disappear upstairs.

By the time he comes back down, it's too late for Sylvie to call. Her aunt and uncle have strict rules. By now it's been . . . can it be? Five full days since they talked. Sylvie doesn't even know about Mama. She doesn't know Perry rescued Flor from the murderous darkness. She doesn't know Flor met the spy girl.

This brings up the question: what doesn't Flor know about Sylvie?

She runs upstairs. An email, she has to send one. The computer is in her parents' room, where Mama's side of the bed is unnaturally smooth. Her brush lies on the bedside table—she forgot it. Her dark hair tangles with Flor's so you can't tell whose is whose. Dad's pillow is on the floor, like he had a one-man pillow fight, and when she picks it up, she gets a whiff of his nighttime smell, that salt-and-bread smell. It turns her into a little kid again, climbing into their big bed to be safe from demons and kidnappers. Safe—that's how easy it used to be to feel safe.

In the corner, the computer's already shut off. The thing is so old, a person could tragically die in the time it takes to boot up. Not that she really wants to email Sylvie, anyway. Flor needs to talk to her. To hear her best friend's voice, her tenderhearted voice, saying the precise, perfect things to make her feel better. Another idea for how to get sent home from

Ridgewood occurs to her. Sylvie can pretend Flor, her lifelong friend, died. It's practically true.

Flor sits on the bed and attempts to channel Sylvie's brain waves. She leans forward, coaxing them across the mainland, over the lake and inside her skull, but all she gets is quiet. It's so quiet, Flor feels alarmed. Is Sylvie sending her a message of peacefulness? Of calm and serenity? Flor jumps up. Is Sylvie telling Flor to feel those things? Or is Sylvie herself feeling peaceful and contented? Flor swallows. Is it possible Sylvie is not thinking of her at all?

In her own room, Thomas occupies ninety-nine percent of her bed. Flor knows she won't be able to sleep, so she takes out the antediluvian copy of *Anne of Avonlea* Mrs. Defoe gave her. About to begin her first teaching job, Anne Shirley bursts with dreams. She wants to awaken the love of beauty in her island students, to stir their young hearts to great things.

Thomas moans in his sleep. When Flor touches his hair, a smile breaks out. His grown-up bottom teeth are coming in crooked. They lean toward one another like they're engaged in a loving, toothy conversation. Flor closes her book and tries to picture an eleven-year-old Mrs. Defoe, reading it, dreaming of becoming an inspiring teacher. Even with an imagination as excellent as Flor's, it's a stretch.

Slipping out of bed, she pushes open her window and sticks her head into the chilly night. The lake is inky black, with a thin drizzle of moonlight. Flor listens to it slap against the rocks. Again, again. That lake! It's so wide, so heartless. It separates her from two of the people she loves best in the world.

So what, says the lake. *Slap. Too bad for you. Slap. What are you gonna do about it? Slap.*

chapter fourteen

Life's a crooked shelf, and things keep rolling off before Flor can catch them. They're out of bread and milk again—who knew they ate and drank so much? Who knew Mama spent half her life going to the store? Flor stops at Two Sisters the next afternoon. The place is empty, except for Queenie, leaning on the counter frowning at her sudoku.

"What's up?" she says to Flor.

"The sun," says Flor.

Every time, they say this.

"How's your mama doing, hon? And your grandma?"

"Okay." Flor sidles down the aisle. Two aisles, that's the whole store, and a cooler. It's Friday, and Island Air doesn't deliver till tomorrow, so all that's left is skim milk.

"She say when she's coming back?"

"Not for sure."

Flor sets the bread and milk jug on the counter. But Queenie doesn't ring them up. Instead she pushes her puzzle aside and shakes her head.

"I remember when my sister left. The first year, I wanted to murder her. I couldn't believe she'd do that to me."

Queenie's sister, Duchess, married the guy from the mainland who installed their new cooler. They live in Cleveland now, though they visit every summer.

"She and I promised each other we'd run this store together till we were little old biddies. We'd have us twin rockers, right there by the postcards. But she up and fell for that devil of a man. I'll tell you, Flor. She wrenched the heart right out of me."

"You can't map the ways of the heart," Flor hears herself say, and Queenie rears back.

"Out of the mouths of babes! It's a good thing you understand that, hon." Her expression goes solemn. "I mean, considering."

"Considering what?"

Queenie goes from solemn to sad. She starts to bag the groceries.

"When you catch a firefly in a jar, you let it go or you keep it. Now which do you think is the better course of action?"

Even the highest-quality grown-ups can ask questions that really . . . why are they wasting everyone's time? But Flor likes Queenie, so she says, "I always let them go."

"Of course you do, hon. And know what? I let Duchess go, and now her and me are back closer than ever." She presses her hands together. "It's different, being separated." She peels them apart. "But love can stretch just as far as you want." She stretches them wide. "Just as far as far as you need it to." Stretches them wider yet.

Flor nods, because she is polite, but that's enough of this strange pantomiming. She reaches for her money, but Queenie refuses to take it. Instead she tucks a couple of packages of Thomas's favorite rainbow-sprinkle doughnuts in the bag and pats Flor's head.

"People have been leaving home as far back as Adam and Eve," she calls as Flor heads out the door.

Back home, when Flor gives Thomas one of the doughnuts, he tears off a piece and offers it to the air around his knees.

"Sit," her brother commands. "Good boy."

"Now what?"

"Paw?" Her brother holds out his hand. His eyebrows disappear up under his hair, and his face floods with delight. "Good boy!"

He's so convincing, Flor almost sees the dog.

He's out the door and into the field, throwing sticks and yelling "Fetch!" It's his own fault they can't have a real dog. Dad would let them in a minute. But when Thomas was three, he pushed gerbil food so far up his nose he had to be life-flighted to the mainland. Thomas enjoyed that helicopter ride so much, Mama's afraid he'd do it again. No more nostril-sized kibble or pellets in this house. No more pets. You'd think the coast was clear, now that he's six, but Mama always says that when it comes to Thomas, an ounce of prevention is worth a pound of cure. She babies that boy—Dad is right. How has she managed to stay away from him this long?

Flor's knees go wishy-washy. Looking down, she realizes she's standing on the spot Mama's feet have worn in the floor in front of the sink. She's fitted her own feet exactly into it.

When did her feet get so big? Another mystery.

Yet another one, though by now it's so normal it might not fit the mystery category: where is Cecilia?

Flor plucks a yellow leaf off the geranium on the windowsill. Whenever she calls Sylvie, she gets the message. She's sent three emails with suggestions, some excellent and some desperate, for ways to get sent home, and Sylvie hasn't replied to a single one.

Another yellow leaf. This plant is dying! No one has watered it since Mama left. Flor sets it in the sink, gently runs the tap over it. She swears she hears that geranium murmur, *You saved me.* It must be terrible to be a house plant. Like being in a zoo. Only a flower pot instead of a cage.

Sylvie won't rebel. Flor knows it. Sylvie doesn't have it in her. She's too soft, too gentle. Always, always, Flor has loved this in her friend, but now?

Now it feels like a betrayal.

The phone rings. Flor grabs it and stares at the number.

"It's you!" she cries.

"It's you!" Sylvie echoes.

"Are you okay? When I tried to channel your brain waves, I got dead air."

"I'm sorry, Flor! It's been cra-cra-craaaazy around here. Saturday I went to this big sleepover party, and then Sunday I was a zombie but my aunt insisted that . . ."

"Wait. You went to a sleepover party?" This is another thing they know about, from TV and movies, but have never experienced for real. "Was it . . . was it fun?"

"Sort of. I was so nervous, I was afraid I'd throw up. I had these babyish polka-dot PJs my mother bought, and everyone else had band T-shirts. Un, again. But then we made these Shrinky Dink necklaces, not the kind where the pieces are already cut out but the kind where you make your own? Everybody liked mine."

This is probably Sylvie-speak for "Everyone went

wildly insane for mine."

"They asked me if I'd make some for them too."

"Wow." The faucet is dripping. Flor gives it a shove.

"I saved the best one for you, Flor."

And then Sylvie tells how they all wore their necklaces to school on Monday, and Mr. Darby, the art teacher, who all the girls think is dreamy, said way cool, and this one girl Blake, who has purple streaks in her hair, not to mention two holes in each ear, said Sylvie was a genius designer, and it just so happened they were starting a clay unit that day, and now Mr. Darby is forcing her to join the art club.

The faucet won't stop dripping. Poking her finger in and out of it, Flor listens. Now and then she gets in an umm, but it's not like Sylvie needs her to say anything.

"Mr. Darby says I have a real feel for three dimensions. And Flor, I know what he means. It's like, reading and math—they just lie there smacked down flat on the page. You know?"

"Not really." Flor spins away from the sink. "When I read something good, it's like I'm right inside it. It's all around me, not flat at all."

"Yeah, but that's you, Flor. That's not me!"

"Well." Flor's spine goes stiff. "I guess that's true." She turns back to peer at the field, where her brother is having a dog hallucination.

"I wish Moonpenny School had art! I mean real art, not cutting out paper snowflakes. We didn't even know what we were missing. We—" She breaks off to speak to someone else for a moment. "I have to go. My aunt signed me up for soccer!"

"What! You hate sports."

"She says soccer will give my self-esteem a boost. Probably it's going to give me a dislocated head."

"Sylvie. Wait. I have to tell you something."

"Okay."

"My mother." Drip. Drip. "She left."

"*What?*"

"I mean, not *left* left. Lita's sick, and she went to help."

"Oh no. Poor Lita!" Sylvie's voice crumples. "Is she going to be okay?"

"It's just bronchitis. You don't die from that."

"Oh, whew. That's good!" Sylvie sighs. "You miss your mom, I know. Everything seems really weird and wrong. You keep thinking she's in the other room, but she's not. Like when the power goes off but you still keep trying to turn on the lights."

"Exactly." Flor sags against the sink. As much as she missed her friend before, it was only a tiny teaspoon of missing compared to right now.

"That's how I felt when I first got here! But your mother had to go! And she misses you too. She loves you and Thomas and Cele more than anything. Just keep telling yourself that."

"You left out my father."

"What?"

"There's another thing. . . ."

"Okay! Okay!" Sylvie calls to her aunt. To Flor she says, "I'll call tomorrow, same time. I promise!"

"Don't break any bones, okay? Or . . . wait. Maybe if you did, they'd send you home. Maybe just a small . . ."

"Must exit." Her alien robot voice. And she's gone.

Flor stares at her big ugly feet. She didn't get to tell about taking that ride with Perry. And he must not have called his sister after all, because Sylvie definitely would have said.

The astonishing fact is, Sylvie didn't utter one word about her brother. For the first time since she left, Perry slipped her mind. A Perry-less mind, that's what Sylvie had. Flor's off the hook. She should be relieved.

So how come she's not?

When she turns back to the window, a new sight meets her eyes. Jasper has appeared out of nowhere, and she's playing with Thomas. Jasper swings her arm, and a stick arcs against the cloud-heavy sky. Jasper does not throw like a girl. Definitely not like a one-handed girl. Thomas races across the grass and bounds back with the stick in his mouth. He goes down on all fours, and Jasper pats his head. Flor bangs out the back door.

"Spit that filthy thing out this second! You'll get worms!"

The stick shoots out of his mouth as quick as if Mama herself stood there scolding.

"That's not likely," says Jasper. This afternoon she wears a knit hat pulled down to her eyes and a tool belt, with hammers and picks and other unidentifiable things dangling like charms on a giant industrial bracelet. "He looks as if he's very familiar with dirt. Besides, his gut's already colonized by millions of microorganisms."

"I can't figure out if you're insulting my brother's gut."

"Why would I do that?" Jasper looks genuinely confused. If she's still offended by Flor, she doesn't act it. She tosses another stick. Her half-empty sleeve swings like a floppy pendulum. Suddenly Thomas morphs back into a boy.

"Where's your arm?" he asks.

Jasper yanks her sweatshirt up over her nose, flicks her eyes from side to side. A trilobite curling up inside its shell, hoping to fool its predators. Flor thinks it again: there cannot be a mother in this picture. A mother would say, *You think you're invisible inside that shirt, but guess what? You're only drawing attention to yourself. And beside, why are you hiding? You're pretty!* A mother would command, *Look, I bought you this nice new shirt in your right size. Put it on this minute.*

"Are you double-jointed?" Thomas asks. "Benjamin, my friend in summer, he could fold his thumb all the way back. It made his mother scream."

"Thomas, what did Mama tell you about asking personal questions?"

"Mama's not here." He flings himself through the tire swing and drags his fingers in the dirt. Jasper's face softens.

"We have that in common," she tells him.

Flor waits for her to say more, but for once Jasper has no info to impart. So Flor flat out asks.

"I've been wondering about that. Where is your mother?"

The corners of Jasper's mouth curve up. "You just told your brother not to—"

"Okay. Right. Sorry."

"You're full of contradictions."

"I am? No, I'm not."

"My mother's in Chile." Jasper's smile fades. "Unless she's already back in Central America."

"What's she doing so far away?"

"She's a renowned paleontologist, specializing in toxodontidae." Jasper peers at the lake. The water's the color of a beat-up pot. "My parents divorced when I was six, and I rarely see her."

"I'm six," says Thomas.

"Statistics show it's better to have two parents. But Father and I adapted nicely." Jasper tugs her hat so low, how can she even see? Between that hat and the oversize clothes, approximately two percent of this girl is visible. "Besides, my mother made a choice, and . . . it wasn't me. It wasn't us."

"Mothers are not allowed to do that."

"I've said it before and I'll say it again. You aren't very observant. My mother did do it!"

"I know, but—"

"When I was small, I required extra care. Even more than the . . . the average child." Jasper pauses. She's busy clearing her throat for quite a while. "Did you know Charles Darwin was the first to uncover toxodon fossils? *Toxodon platensis* lived during the Pleistocene period and resembled a hippo or rhino, with a large snout and curved teeth. Its habitat was South America, and its study requires travel to remote terrain." She tugs her hat even lower. "You know who Charles Darwin was."

"I said I did." Flor puts her hands in her pockets. "But I don't."

"He sailed around the world on the H.M.S. *Beagle*, exploring and collecting specimens. Back in the eighteen hundreds, most people believed that God was done creating, but Darwin proved that new species appear all the time. For example, he found that the finches of the Galápagos Islands, who all started out the same, evolved to have different kinds of beaks. Fat beaks, thin beaks, curved or straight beaks, depending on what they needed to survive and flourish. For example, some ate seeds. But others . . ."

Flor only half listens. How could Jasper's mother choose prehistoric roadkill over her and Dr. Fife? Her heart must be cold. Colder than the swim hole. What mother abandons her family for any reason whatsoever in this world? Flor watches her brother drag his feet and hands in the filthy dirt.

"She made a huge mistake." She interrupts Jasper. "I mean, colossal. Your renowned mother."

"I'll take that as a compliment." The sun breaks through a cloud, and Jasper's ginger-ale-colored hair fizzes in the light. "Thank you."

"Maybe she'll change her mind and come back."

"It's been five years."

"Still!"

"All evidence is to the contrary. Your hypothesis is not supported."

How strange she is! Like one of those kids raised in a forest by wolves. Only for her, it's a white-bearded guy in love with extinct creatures. Jasper picks up a rock, flips it with a quick jab of her chin, judges it worthless, and tosses it away.

"Charles Darwin was shy. He preferred to observe the world rather than have it observe him." She leans down to scratch Thomas's head. "Good dog!"

"Ruff ruff!"

She clanks out of sight.

chapter fifteen

Cecilia still isn't home at suppertime. Never, ever has she been late without calling. "What kind of teenager is so good?" Mama always teased. "Just once, be bad! *¡Vaya, sea malita!* Break some rules! Have a little fun!"

People should be careful what they wish for.

The three of them are staring glumly at their meatballs, which to tell the truth taste of freezer burn. Thomas puts one on the floor for his dog, and Dad doesn't even notice. When the phone rings, Flor races to answer.

"Tell him I'm studying with Lauren Long." Click. Cecilia's gone.

"Cele's studying with Lauren Long."

"See?" Dad gets up to clear the table. "Nothing to worry about. Not with our Saint Cele."

Could he be more aggravating? Doesn't he notice who cooked the spaghetti? Who, when Cecilia still doesn't appear, forces Thomas to peel off his clothes, only to discover that he's wearing three sets of underpants on top of each other, his translation of "put on clean underwear"? Who makes him get in a tub that immediately turns the color of ditch water? Does their father have eyes in his head? If he isn't careful, Flor will begin to yell at him, just like Mama did.

Does.

It's raining, but when Cecilia finally comes home, she's dry as dry can be. Beyond dry—she's a pile of kindling that will burst into flame at the hint of a match. Studying with Lauren must have been very stimulating. Dad asks if she's hungry, further proof he has no clue, because when was the last time he saw Cecilia eat, really eat? He actually looks sympathetic when she groans that she still has a ton of homework,

150

heads for her closet, and shuts the door.

Only Flor seems to notice that it's Friday night. Or that her backpack full of books still sits on the kitchen floor.

The rain is mean. Mean like cruel and mean like this means change is coming. Flor's still awake, listening to it throw itself against the windows, when Dad climbs the stairs. Within minutes, the *ffft ffft* of his snoring blends with the sound of the rain.

For once Thomas is in his own bed, and her room's so lonesome it's like even she isn't there. Dragging her pillow and covers out onto the landing, she opens her book. Anne Shirley's having trouble with one of her boy students, but it breaks her heart to discipline him. Anne makes so many mistakes herself! She's always rushing headlong, and feeling things with trembling intensity, and letting her imagination run completely, insanely wild. She reads her students fairy tales and takes them rambling through the woods. Mrs. Defoe could take a lesson here.

"De foe," Joe called her today. "De opposite of de friend."

The rain is on a mission to soak every inch of the

island. Flor thinks of Joe and Jocelyn and the many Hawkinses crammed into their falling-down house. She thinks of Mrs. Defoe, asleep between brown sheets. Thinks of Jasper and Dr. Fife in their room with the slanted roof, their beds like islands in a sea of fossils. She thinks of Jasper's mother, camped out in some remote forest, and of Charles Darwin, sailing from one exotic, rocky island to another. Finches. What did Jasper say about finches?

She won't think about Mama. Won't.

Huddled in her pile of covers, Flor's an island herself. The rain is the sea, slapping her shores, washing over her rocks. Is that a boat on the horizon, sails rustling, a woman peering at her through a telescope? The woman waves. She murmurs Flor's name.

"Flor."

When Flor opens her eyes, her sister's face is an inch away.

"Aren't you starving?" Cele whispers. "Come on."

They tiptoe down the stairs. Cecilia snaps on the kitchen light and starts pulling things out of the fridge. Plops a chunk of butter in a skillet. Cracks four eggs, whisks them with cream. As the eggs sizzle,

152

she throws in cheese and shakes on the hot sauce they both love. Her wrist is a perfect golden hinge. After days of unrelenting tomato sauce, the smell is so delicious Flor can hardly stand it. You'd think they'd wake their father, but nothing ever does. "That's the sleep of a man with a clean conscience," Mama says.

Toast. More butter. The delectable rose-hip jelly Two Sisters sells at the end of summer. They don't even bother with plates but eat right out of the skillet. Cecilia shovels it in like a girl who hasn't eaten in forever. The two of them together. It feels nice. It feels so snug and nice. Cecilia smiles at Flor.

"Thanks for covering for me."

Mouth gluey with toast, Flor shakes her head. Cecilia sets down her fork.

"You didn't?"

"I just told him what you said."

The wet, black window reflects two close-together heads. One—the pretty one—draws back.

"Right," says Cele. "Good."

"It was the truth, right?"

Cecilia picks up her fork and fills her mouth with egg.

"Because," says Flor, "Mama's not here, and Lita's sick, and this family needs to stick together. People shouldn't be taking advantage of the situation."

"Yeah, well." Cecilia stabs a lump of egg. "Mama doesn't seem to care a whole lot about sticking together."

Flor sits back, shocked. "She had to go! She—"

"Flor, there are ten million relatives who live right there. Mama could've come back by now if she really wanted to." Cecilia points her fork. "All that food in the freezer? She's been planning this. She was just waiting for a good excuse."

Flor almost falls out of her chair.

"Planning what? What are you talking about?"

"Some people just aren't cut out to live here." Cecilia pushes the frying pan away. "Some people need a different kind of life."

"Not Mama!" An icy, invisible finger taps Flor's forehead. "Mama likes to cook. She got carried away in the cooking department, that's all."

"Maybe."

Tap tap. Cold seeps into Flor's brain. "Are you saying she really left? Because she would've said. She definitely would've told us."

154

"Unless she wasn't sure herself."

"You're making this up! Your hypothesis is not supported."

Cecilia takes the pan to the sink, runs hot water. She scrubs hard, just like Mama. Her back to Flor, she says, "When I was little, Moonpenny was the world and the world was Moonpenny. Like playing Town, remember? Remember how fun that game was?"

Does she forget who she's talking to? Of course Flor remembers!

"Like the center of the universe," Cecilia says. "That's how home feels, when you're little."

She turns around. A strand of black hair sticks to her glowing cheek. Flor's gotten used to seeing that face shut to her, but now it's open, a beautiful flung-open window. Happy and sad mix together there, but mostly happy. Flor shrinks back in her chair.

"Maybe you'll turn out like Dad," her big sister says. "Maybe you'll live here in perfect contentment your whole life. That'd be nice. That'd be good. But everybody's not made the same."

"I know that," Flor whispers.

"Even people who start out from the same place,

155

they can go in different directions. They can change. They can . . . they can discover they want something very different from what they thought."

Cecilia reaches for a towel and slowly dries her hands. First one, then the other, then the first one again, like her hands are precious objects. The overhead light makes a halo on her dark hair, but Cecilia's not a saint. That is a new thought. Flor grips her chair.

"Cele, please tell me where you were tonight."

Her sister folds the dish towel so each corner is perfectly squared, then hangs it up. "Come on. It's late."

This is not an answer. This is like an adult with a dried-up heart saying *It's okay. You'll get used to it.*

Flor turns her head. She won't look as Cecilia walks out of the room.

Alone at the table, Flor's bare feet are ice cubes. The room's not cozy anymore. The night on the other side of the window is big and dark. Flor feels it pressing against the glass, trying hard to get in.

chapter sixteen

All week, Flor tries her best to turn Cecilia into
a book so high up on a shelf you can't reach it.
She tries to fold her sister small and flat and put her
in the very back of the drawer. If Cecilia wants a sister
divorce, fine. Fine with her!

Friday night, Dad announces he's going to Toledo
tomorrow.

"Can I come?" says Thomas.

"Not this time, old buddy."

He catches the first ferry. Flor's up to say good-
bye, and when he hugs her, she presses her cheek hard

against his broad chest, like he's a wishing fossil.

Bring her back.

That day she does laundry, and scrubs the kitchen floor, and makes Thomas stay in the bath till he's wrinkled as a little old man. Cecilia actually hangs around, though the way she pouts and moons, Flor almost wishes she'd go.

"I just hope you're not counting on her," says Cecilia.

"Never mind what I'm counting on," says Flor, but a second later can't help adding, "You'll see."

Does Cecilia even care? Whatever she's up to, she'd never get away with it if Mama was here. Mama is eagle-eyed. She sees enough for two, which must be why Dad sees nothing. No wonder Cecilia hopes Mama stays away.

That is such a terrible thought, such a treacherous, traitorous thought, Flor has to sit down for a while.

By late afternoon, there's nothing left to do. Thomas wears clothes fresh from the dryer. Flor won't let him off the porch, where he sits whispering secret commands to Petey, the invisible dog.

"Roll over. Paw. Good boy!"

Mama says prayer isn't asking for things. That's wishing, she says. Mama! Put all her opinions together, you'd get a book fatter than the Bible. Real prayer is simply talking to God, Mama says. It's opening wide your reverent, humble heart.

Sitting on the porch swing, eyes closed and hands folded, Flor tries. But within three seconds, she's reverently, humbly begging. Cecilia's head pokes out the door.

"Dad texted. He's on the next ferry."

They, he meant.

Flor takes her little brother's hand.

"Let's go," she says. "They're coming."

The two of them have gotten as far as the abandoned farmhouse when Cecilia catches up. Not a word out of her. But that's okay. Possibly even better. She's here with them. That's what matters.

For a person used to galloping everywhere, walking feels strange. Flor likes to ride fast, turning the scenery into a bright ribbon getting wound onto a spool. But today she knows: it's her moving, not the world. Her moving through the world.

159

Thomas runs ahead, waits for them, runs ahead again. Cecilia refuses to speed up or speak. It's like she thinks she's in a solemn procession. Flor's so grateful her sister's with them, she buttons her own lip.

The clock tower pokes up against the sky . . . 11:16. Flor jerks her head, refusing to acknowledge the stupid frozen thing.

The afternoon is golden. The golden leaves, the goldenrod, the golden honeybees, the golden air itself. The sun drops golden doubloons of light in a shimmering line all across to the mainland. Anybody with eyes in her head would fall in love with Moon-penny today. Anyone would step off the ferry and think, I'm so glad I'm home! Why would I ever want to leave this place?

Mama gets seasick, so she never stands on deck, always stays in the car. When the *Patricia Irene* draws close enough that they can make out Dad, alone at the rail, it doesn't mean anything. Not a thing.

Flor curls her fingers around the dock's thick iron chain. The last time she was here, Sylvie left. That day is like a fossil. Like something flattened and buried.

160

Cecilia comes to stand beside her. Her pinkie hooks Flor's.

She cares.

Thunk. The ferry docks. The gulls on the pilings all lift off at the precise same moment. How do they do that?

The few cars rolling off are crammed to the roof. Now's the time the islanders lay in the last supplies for the long winter ahead. Fifty-pound bags of cat food, toilet paper for an army. Big blocks of clay for Delia Blackenberry, the sculptor, extra pens and boxes of paper for Betty Magruder, who spends deep winter nights writing epic poems about tragic shipwrecks.

Their car's the last one off. Thomas swings his fat arms up, touchdown style. But a moment later, they flop back to his sides. Dad rolls down the car window and tries for a smile.

"A welcoming committee! How do you like that. Hop in, *chicos.*"

Cecilia flings herself into the empty front passenger seat. Flor and Thomas climb in the back.

"Where's Mama?" Thomas glances around like she might be hiding under the seat or in the trunk.

Any second she'll pop out. Surprise!

"Buddy, she's still with Lita and Tia Aurora and everybody else. It wasn't . . . wasn't time for her to come home yet." Dad looks at them in the rearview mirror. "She sent you all lots of hugs."

"You can keep mine," says Cecilia.

"She's counting on you, Cecilia." Dad turns in his seat. He lowers his voice. "You most of all."

"Where's Mama?" Thomas still thinks saying something over and over will make it happen.

Dad stares out the windshield and forgets to drive. Flor rarely views her father from behind, and she sees how wide his shoulders are, how broad his neck. Mama's barely half his size, but if he ran away and left them, she'd make him come back. She'd see justice done. Anger settles inside Flor. Like she swallowed a hot coal, it burns inside her. He let her go! How could he do that?

"Everything okay, chief?" Tim the ferry guy leans down to Dad's window.

"Huh? Oh, yeah. Sure thing!" Dad's grin is so artificial, can't Tim see? Is the man blind? Or does he see and pretend not to, and isn't that worse? How exactly is that different from lying?

"Bea okay?" Tim says.

"You bet. Just fine." Dad pulls out into the road. "Thanks for asking!"

"Where's Mama?" Thomas refuses to surrender. "Hey, Dad?"

"Stop the car." Cecilia's voice makes a fist.

"What?" Dad grips the wheel. He darts Cele a quick look. "You're upset, sure you are. But you just gotta hold on here, and be patient. You—"

"I said stop the car!"

Dad jams on the brake. Cecilia yanks open her door and jumps out.

"You think pretending makes it better?" she cries.

"Cele." Dad suddenly looks way older than when he left this morning. He looks like Dad disguised as an eighty-year-old man. "What are you doing? Get back in the car right now."

"You adults! You're all enormous fakes! You're a bunch of liars!"

"Get back in this car. You're being disrespectful!"

"Don't tell me what I am!"

Slam. Cele's running. Long legs flashing, black

163

hair streaming. Running, running, running away.

"What's she doing?" Dad turns to Flor. "Where's she going?"

How's Flor supposed to know? All she knows is she'd rather look at anything than her father's stricken, suddenly old face. Throwing open her door, she tumbles out into the road. Cecilia's got a head start, and who knew she could run that fast in those boots?

"Cele! Stop!"

Her sister speeds up. In desperation Flor pumps her arms, lifts her knees.

"Stop!"

But Cecilia keeps getting smaller. And now Flor feels herself shrinking too. Something whittles away at her, scraping off bits and more bits, pieces of her flying off, till all that's left is her heart, exposed to the air and light, nothing at all to protect it. Nothing to shield it from the bitter, biting truth.

"You were right!" Flor calls. "About Mama! Cele! Come back!"

Something hooks the toe of her shoe, the road tilts beneath her, and she's flopping on the ground like a hooked fish. Dirt between her teeth. Elbows and palms scraped raw. A touch on the back of her hand makes her lift her head. A ragged paw pokes through the grass at the side of the road.

"Owww," says Flossie Magruder.

Out on the bay, the *Patricia Irene* chugs back to the mainland. The first thing Flor ever wanted to be was a ferry-boat captain. She wanted to blow the ship horn and twirl that big wooden wheel. But lying here, she feels sorry for the captain. She feels sorry for the old *Patricia Irene* itself, chugging back and forth, back and forth, never getting anywhere.

Cecilia's disappeared. Right before Flor's eyes.

"Owww," Flossie Magruder says again, and that's when Flor starts to cry.

chapter seventeen

Fly, Misty! Fly like the western wind!

Flor slides her feet into the stirrups and swings up into the saddle. She needs to gallop. Needs to move fast, even if she has no idea where she's going.

But something happens. No—nothing happens. Flor leans forward, but her bike remains a bike. Its cold metal refuses to warm, to ripple and come alive. Squeaky wheels, not clip-clopping hooves. No long, flowing mane or soft answering neigh.

Misty? Where are you, girl?

Flor rides faster, hardly caring where she is going.

She races along Lilac Lane, past the Hawkinses' house, its mountain range of junk gleaming in the Sunday-morning light. Doubles back and swings up onto Shore Road. Doesn't stop as she passes the turnoff for the neck, the quiet airstrip. The milkweed pods have gone gray and papery. Fallen leaves spatter the road. Misty? Misty! Veers around the front of the island, past the ferry landing. Where are you? The distant mainland lies like a wrinkled old sock. Zooms right past Two Sisters.

It's no use. Misty is gone. She headed for the hills when Flor wasn't looking.

Flor has to stop. She's out of breath. A flock of birds, a hundred or more, wings overhead, on their way north toward the open lake. The flock breaks into separate bits, some birds going one way, some another. She keeps watching, waiting for them to get it back together, but the last she sees of them, that flock is still messed up and confused.

A golf cart's weaving merrily along the road. It screeches to a stop beside her.

"Just in time!" Dr. Fife's face lights up like a scoreboard after a home run. He and Jasper wear their father-daughter tool belts. "We're on our way to the field and could use a third pair of hands. Hop in, Miss F and F!"

It'll only be two and a half pairs of hands, Flor thinks, knowing it's a mean thought, and what makes Dr. Fife so sure she has nothing else to do? Jasper shifts in her seat, clinking and clanking with embarrassment. She's too old for her father to be finding her playmates.

But now she's turning around, moving equipment so Flor can fit in the backseat, and now Flor's ditching her bike, and here they go, hurtling toward Moonpenny Quarry. Let it be recorded, Dr. Fife is the worst driver on the face of the Earth. He brakes for nothing, then speeds up like somebody's giving away hundred-dollar bills and they have thirty seconds to get there. Forget backing up. By the time they get to the quarry, Flor's stomach thinks it went to Cedar Point Amusement Park.

"Our brains are made of very soft tissue," Jasper whispers. "Good thing our skulls are so hard." She knocks hers with her fist, and Flor laughs.

Down in the quarry, all Dr. Fife's goofiness

168

vanishes. It's like a fairy tale where the bear's mangy old hide falls away, and out steps the shining prince. He produces picks and chisels and hammers. Brushes and Sharpies and balls of twine.

"Trilobites inhabited Earth approximately three times as long as dinosaurs," he tells Flor, in case she's wondering. It's easy to see where Jasper got her lecturing tendencies. "Think of it! They rode along when the continents drifted! They made themselves at home in arctic and tropic waters. They were there as mountain chains rose and landmasses sank. Humans will be doing well to last a fraction as long."

Flor has to admit, he's good. Listen to him for a few minutes, and you want to be a trilobite cheerleader too. You too are convinced those little guys were heroes.

"I hope the weather holds." He squints at the sky. "In another couple of weeks, Jasper and I will have enough specimens to keep us busy all through the winter."

Jasper rolls up both her XXL sleeves. *Tap tap tap.* The two Fifes work slowly, painstakingly, happily. *Tap tap tap.* Minuscule splinters of stone fall away.

With a small brush, Dr. Fife tenderly sweeps aside the slivers, and Jasper gathers them in a ziplock bag she keeps clamped to her side. It's impossible two hands could be quicker or surer than her one. *Tap. Tap tap.* Now a magnifying glass, and the two of them make a thoughtful inspection before he chisels away more rock.

Flor might as well have vaporized, but she doesn't mind. Quarry quiet. It's so personal. Like, if Mother Earth has a brain, she's giving you a peek inside, letting you read her thoughts. Not just the ones on top, the everyday thoughts she shares with everyone, but the private ones. The ones she usually keeps to herself, all hidden and secret.

If you want to be truly alone. If you want the rest of the world to stop hurting you, stop confusing you and knocking you around. Here's where you should come.

But before long, Dr. Fife walks over to where Flor perches on a rock. His eyes twinkle.

"This is where we are." He points to a spot on a hand-drawn map. "And this is where I want to dig next. Why do I have the feeling you're good at measuring?"

170

Before she can answer, he's handing her a ball of twine, scissors, and a measuring tape.

"Jasper will tell you what to do," he says.

"Oh, I'm sure."

They both glance toward where Jasper is busy sweeping up rock dust.

"She's glad to have you for a friend, Flor," he says quietly. He looks at Flor in a way that reminds her of her own father, who understands some things so well and others not at all. He gives his white beard a tug. "She doesn't meet many other young people. That always seemed to suit her just fine, but lately . . ." Another tug, like he's trying to pull the thoughts out. "This past year, I'm afraid she's been a little . . ."

"Lonesome?"

"You've put your finger on it. In fact, if I had to quantify it, I'd say she's been more than a little lonesome. Perhaps even very."

Jasper looks up, like she senses they're talking about her. This is embarrassing. Flor jumps down, takes the map from Dr. Fife.

"Who knew we'd meet a unique specimen like you, Miss Flora and Fauna?" Dr. Fife smiles and clasps his hands. "We came hunting trilobites and found you too. It's life at its most glorious, unpredictable best!"

Wait.

"I thought science was all about predictable," Flor says.

"Scientists love having our expectations overturned! We delight in the unanticipated. That's where we make our most valuable discoveries."

Flor's never met an adult happy about what he didn't know. Scientists are their own species, this is clear.

"Can I ask something?" she says.

"Please!"

"Is sight still evolving? I mean, will future humans be able to see miles away? Or through walls? Or in the dark?"

"A fascinating question." More beard tugging. "I don't know the answer, Flor. But I do know one thing for sure. We humans could always get better at seeing. How often do we look at something, yet only see the surface? Or what we expect to see? Sometimes we even refuse to see what's right before us." Tug tug. "I've always disliked that saying 'There's more than meets the eye.' Everything is visible, if only we know how to look. Truly seeing is the first step to truly understanding. Sometimes I think that's why we were put on Earth—to see as much as we can, as clearly as we can."

Flor's brain turns this over as she and Jasper measure out a new grid, closer to the swim hole. She steadies the stakes while Jasper drives them in with sure, one-handed whacks. The sun rolls up the hill of blue sky, spills down into the rocky craters and cracks. Dr. Fife's map shows every one of them. On a regular map, Moonpenny is just a dot, a titch, a pinch. On your usual map, the lake is so enormous it could swallow the island in one gulp.

But the map in her hand is different. *Every square inch of the island is important,* says this map. *Pay attention to each stone, each patch of dirt,* says this map. *Who knows what you'll see. What's under your own two big feet.* What Jasper said, that very first day they met, echoes inside Flor: *There's plenty to see. You live here—shouldn't you know that?*

"Hey," Flor hears herself say. "Thank you."

"You're welcome." Jasper frowns. "For what?"

"I don't know. I've been coming to this quarry my whole life, but it's like I never really saw it."

"That's good. But why thank me? You're developing your own powers of observation."

This girl does not tell lies. She may be the only person Flor ever met who doesn't.

Except Sylvie, of course.

"Jasper, you could just say you're welcome, you know."

Flor lays the map on the ground and anchors it with a smooth yellow rock. They measure out another square. The afternoon's warm, and Jasper pushes back her hair with her ABS arm. Flor's almost used to that arm by now. There may be some things Jasper can't do, but so far, don't ask Flor to name them. Another square. They're working hard. They make a good team.

"It must've been so bizarre to get the first eyes," says Flor. "Like in the beginning, maybe things would be blurry and shadowy, like looking through out-of-focus binoculars. Or like when you just wake up and your eyes are full of sleep till you rub them. Or like when you pull at their corners so things go mushy."

She demonstrates. Jasper laughs.

"Or maybe it was like looking out through a curtain, and very, very slowly it got thinner and thinner till it finally disintegrated and then one day, wow! There was nothing but perfectly clear transparent glass, and the trilobites could see the whole world, all colorful and beautiful and terrifying at the same time." Flor windmills her arms. "That must have boggled their tiny trilobite brains. Did they even have brains?"

"A rudimentary system."

"Like my brother's."

"Sight took eons to evolve. We still don't know for sure how it all unfolded."

Flor deflates. *Sssss.* Sylvie would've jumped in with her own theories, and by now they'd be stumbling around pretending to see trees and rocks and deer poop for the first time. But Jasper? Negative imagination. What you see is what you get with this girl.

Then Jasper says, "You're like a trilobite yourself."

"What!" cries Flor.

"Didn't you just say you're seeing this quarry for the first time?"

Dr. Fife is waving to them.

"Flor, Jasper, my little guppies! Come look!"

Bulging from the face of the limestone is something that resembles a miniature mummy case. He waves his hammer.

"Back at my lab, we'll do a CT scan and find out everything there is to know. But that's nothing compared to this moment. This is the best part, isn't it, Jasper? Nothing sets a geologist's heart pounding like the initial discovery. We've found something, but what? Is it just a fragment, or the tip of something much bigger? Is it a species we already know, or something never before seen?"

Dr. Fife's excitement is contagious. The rocks! The silent rocks! He knows how to make them speak. He knows how to hear them when they do.

"Our friend has waited in the very same spot for millions of years. Humans and animals have walked past her, sat on her, never knowing she was there. But now we've found her." His eyes are candlelit, like Thomas's. "Or, as I like to think, she's found us."

He does something surprising. He sets one hand on Flor's shoulder and the other on Jasper's.

"Little nestlings, let's honor the moment," he says. "Let's make it last a bit longer."

So they stand there, not saying a word, and it's nice. Flor half closes her eyes, and the air flickers to life. Strange, spiny fish flash their silver fins. Pearly seashells encrust the rocks, and enormous translucent jellyfish drift by. The creature in the rock is still alive, busy being who she is, living in her world. Flor's world now. The rocks link them all, then to now, life to life.

The world is so big. And so small. It makes you dizzy. Flor opens her eyes.

"Ready?" Another gentle tap, and the fossil is in Dr. Fife's hand. "Aah. *Phacops rana*. The leader of the humble, the mighty trilobites."

Pulling out a magnifying glass, he gives Flor a guided tour. He shows her how the body has three parts, hence the *tri*. The thorax is made of tiny joints, so it can roll itself into a ball.

"It's articulated," says Jasper, Namer of All Things.

"Right there?" says Dr. Fife. "That's her head. And these are her eyes. What resemble dozens of pins all lined up? Actually lenses. Pixels, if you like. If our friend were alive, she'd be staring back at us with crystal-clear vision. And, no doubt, with enormous surprise."

He chuckles fondly, as if he and the gazillion-year-old creature really are best buds. Setting the fossil in Flor's hand, he gently cups her fingers around it.

"For you."

"For real?"

Like a diamond in the sky—thus Dr. Fife's eyes.

Afterward, they drive Flor back to where they picked her up. There's her bike, leaning against a tree. An old, tired tree. Its roots stick up like bent, gnarly knees. Her bike? Obviously, it's a bike, not a horse. Here is the trouble with observing closely. The happiness Flor felt in the quarry drains away.

"Are you okay?" Dr. Fife and Jasper twist around to face her. Their heads tilt at the precise same angle.

Flor feels like she swallowed a fish hook. If she tells them about Mama, they won't understand. They'll think they do, because Mrs. Fife left too, but how can they possibly? Their family is different from hers. Their family is odd and strange. Jasper will recite a scientific fact, one that is fully supported. Her father will tug his beard. The two of them inhabit their own exotic desert Island of Fife.

"I'm okay," says Flor.

"You look pale," says Dr. Fife.

"She always looks like that," says Jasper.

Flor climbs out. Jasper watches with those penetrating green eyes, eyes that miss exactly nothing. Flor might as well be under that magnifying glass. Jasper knows Flor's not okay. But she doesn't know what to do about it. Flor's heart twists. Who does she feel worse for, herself or Jasper? It doesn't matter. There's no room in her life to worry about anyone else. She grabs her bike.

"Thanks for everything," she says.

At home, Thomas rushes to her, his face panicked.

"Where'd you go?" he demands.

Why should she tell her little brother where she was? It's her life!

"To the store."

She's getting like Cele! No. No she is not.

"Then where's the food?"

"Look." She grabs her backpack and pulls out the treats she carries for Violet's dog. "I got this for Petey!"

Thomas bursts out crying. The tears cut tracks down his grubby cheeks.

"Petey's lost! I can't find him no place!"

Flor finally notices—the house is a wreck. The couch and chair cushions are on the floor. The kitchen cupboards stand open, pots and pans strewn around. Somebody yanked every coat and jacket out of the hall closet and tossed around the winter boots. *How can you tell?* she wants to ask her brother. *How do you know when something invisible disappears?*

"Did you look upstairs?" she hears herself say.

"I looked every place!" Thomas mashes his face into her stomach. "He ran away!"

"No," she says, stroking his hair. "Petey would never! He loves you!"

They sit on the rug, Thomas in her lap. Shaking the bag of treats, Flor softly calls, "Petey! Petey, where are you, boy?"

Misty, where are you, girl?

Mama?

Sylvie?

Cele?

"Petey!" She tightens her arm around her brother.

Her voice trembles as she calls, louder and louder. "Come on home, old Pete! What do you think you're doing? Come on back right now, you hear? Right now!"

"I think I hear him," Thomas whispers. He leans forward. "You hear him, Flor?"

"I think so. Yes, for sure I do."

Those tiny candles flicker in his big brown eyes.

"He's here!" Thomas leaps off her lap and tears out the door. But a moment later he's back, pressing his snotty cheek against hers.

"You're never going away, right?" he says.

Who does he think he's talking to?

chapter eighteen

Flor's book report is due tomorrow and she's barely halfway through *Anne of Avonlea*. For the first time in her life, she has trouble reading. Her mind skids this way and that, so she reads the same sentence a dozen times and still has no idea what it says. This is how reading always is for Sylvie. This is why she'd much rather arrange books into towers than read them.

Last night, she sent Flor a long email. They only talk about once a week now, because Sylvie is so busy dodging soccer balls and being the star of the art club and learning to speak French like a Parisian mademoiselle. It's better, they agreed, to write emails. Sylvie's have a million typos and mistakes. She's always been a disastrous speller, but last night, Flor could tell she wrote with approximately one-eighth of her brain.

Plus, the font was bright green instead of purple.

Still, a couple of lines made Flor smile.

Like: "I finely went for a bike ride. My cosin's bike is a mule not a wild horse."

And: "I got contacts! I can see to the sides now not just strait ahead. Why didn't you tell me the world is so wide?"

Every day, Flor sends another suggestion for getting sent home from Ridgewood. It's hopeless, but she won't give up. "You are so stubborn!" Mama always tells her. "It's your weakness and your strength, Florita!"

She takes *Anne of Avonlea* outside at recess. She's going to have to skim it, and her report's going to be a disaster. Sitting on a bench, she skips ahead to one of her favorite parts, where Anne, who's expecting important company, intends to rub her nose with antifreckle lotion but by mistake smears on scarlet red dye. Anne of accidents! Flor laughs out loud.

"What's so funny?"

Joe Hawkins stands beside her. Weighing a good-sized rock in each hand.

"Don't do it," says Flor.

But he does. *Bonk.* The first rock bounces off the face of the clock and lands in the grass.

"If Mrs. Defoe catches you, your head is history."

Joe shrugs. The second rock bounces off the face of the clock—*plonk*—and rolls back at their feet. Joe scowls at the tower like it attacked him instead of vice versa.

"I'm not sure what you're trying to do," she says. "But I'm pretty sure it's not working."

"Time's not supposed to stand still," he says, still scowling. "It's supposed to march on."

What is this? He's sitting down beside her. Pulling a piece of sandpaper out of his pocket, attacking a splinter sticking up between them on the bench. Flor closes her book.

"I don't think bombing the clock will fix it," she says.

Jocelyn appears, taps them each with her wand

three times, and canters away.

"But I wish somebody would," Flor goes on. "Fix it, I mean. Because these days, every time I look at it, I swear I hear it say, *Na na the boo boo. Nothing's going to change, so just get used to it.*"

For sure Joe will shrug.

But no.

"I *know* how to fix it." He'll sand straight through the bench if he keeps it up. "Anyway, I think I do."

"Really?"

"Ow." His finger got a sliver. He scowls at it too. He's a scowling machine. "You know anything about that clock?"

"My father says it's right twice a day."

"Yeah, well, my father says people used to set their watches by it. They were really proud of it, back in the day. It was like a symbol of the island. People used to get their pictures taken in front of it."

"Like in those old photos outside the office," says Flor. "Mrs. Defoe's in some of them. She has long curly hair! But you can still tell it's her."

"A clock guy came over from Cleveland every year to inspect it and clean it. My father would go up there with him and watch. From up there, you can see across the lake in every direction."

Jocelyn is back. She wiggles onto the bench between them, sticks her feet straight out in front of her. Joe pretends to sandpaper her head. A small brown bird lands on the clock's hour hand and starts to sing. A big song, for such a pipsqueak bird. Is it a finch?

"My dad says what's wrong could be simple as a worn-out spring. Or maybe one of the weights fell off. He says by now, rain and wind have damaged the wood so bad, it's letting in moisture and causing more damage."

"Daddy is super smart," says Jocelyn, folding her hands in her lap.

"When the island hit hard times, they quit hiring the clock expert," Joe goes on. "The clock slowed down and finally stopped. My dad told the village council he'd watched the guy for years, and he knew he could fix it. He practically begged them to give him the chance. But Mayor Pinch? That sack of cow manure said no."

"That sack of cow manure!" shouts Jocelyn.

"But that's so stupid," Flor says. "Why wouldn't they let—"

"Because." His voice pitches so low, she has to lean across Jocelyn to hear. "They said they don't want him climbing up there. They don't trust . . . He might . . ."

Flor looks back at the tower. It's high. Steep, narrow steps or a ladder—however you got up there, you'd need to be careful. Watch your step. Keep your balance. Have all your wits about you. Her bad dream wings over her, plunging her into its shadow.

"Oh," she says softly.

"Hey." Thomas gets into the act, squeezing his way onto the bench next to Jocelyn, who kicks him. He kicks her back. They're having a wonderful time. Joe speaks to Flor over their heads.

"But if I went up there with him, I could, you know. Keep an eye on him. I've watched every YouTube ever made on how old clocks work." He crumples the sandpaper in his fist. "Between him and me, we could get it going. I know we could."

"That'd be great. That'd be a service to the whole island."

"Right?" He pounds his fist on his knee. "And maybe when people looked up at it, they'd think, *Huh. What do you know. Look what those trashy Hawkinses did.*"

"We're not trashy!" yells Jocelyn.

"Yes, you are!" yells Thomas.

They're off, chasing each other across the grass.

"Your dad needs to ask again," Flor says. "He shouldn't give up. Nobody should, but especially not parents!"

Joe's shoulders start to lift, but Flor pushes them back down.

"You shrug too much."

Joe's eyes go wide. Flor snatches her hands away and hides them behind her back. Like *that* never happened.

Except that, all through the afternoon, her hands keep remembering the bony-soft feel of him. Untouching him is impossible. Impossible.

Covered casseroles and plates of cookies and brownies pile up on their kitchen table, like after a funeral. Platters of fried chicken, bowls of butterscotch pudding, canning jars of pickles and tomatoes and plums. Queenie has organized a rotating list of cooks, and when Dad says it's not necessary, she says her left foot it isn't. With all he does for the island, the least they can do is help him and the kids out in their own hour of need!

Dad tells Flor, Cele, and Thomas that they're not in need. Have they got that? They're just fine. But you never insult people who want to help. Remember that, kids.

How often do we look at something and not really see it?

Flor has to talk to Mama. Not just for a few minutes, with the rest of the family eavesdropping, but alone. *People are acting like you died,* she'll say. *They're treating us like half orphans.* When Mama hears that, she'll get so upset, she'll get so angry, she'll jump on the next ferry. And if that doesn't work, Flor will move on to precious baby Thomas. *He's scooting around the house on his bottom, claiming he forgets how to walk. Also, his bed is full of dog biscuits. Also, Dad promised to take him target shooting.* This last isn't true, but so what.

189

And if all that fails, there is Cecilia. *She's sneaking around, Mama. I know you don't believe me, but it's true. That's how bad things are here. That's how upside down and inside out, Mama!*

Obviously she can't say any of this while standing in the kitchen. She's got to talk to Mama in private, but how? Cecilia never lets her cell phone out of her sight. And Flor doesn't know anyone . . .

Wait. Yes she does.

She finds Jasper sitting on the porch of the Red Robin Inn, her nose in a book. When she looks up, she's so startled to see Flor, the book slips from her hand and slides onto the floor. Flor picks it up. A biography of Charles Darwin.

"You really love this guy, don't you?"

"Guess what. He almost didn't become a scientist. His father made him go to medical school. But that was back before they invented anesthesia, and the first time he saw an operation, with buckets of blood and the patient shrieking, Darwin ran out and fainted. Then his father tried to force him to be a minister, but he wasn't any good at that either."

"Parents!"

"Thank goodness he followed his true heart." Jasper tugs the hem of her giant sweatshirt and gives a shy smile. "You came here."

She looks so pleased. Flor swallows.

"I wanted to . . . Can I ask you a favor? Can I borrow your cell phone?"

"Oh. Sure." Jasper stands up too quickly. "It's upstairs."

Flor follows her up. The room is even more of a catastrophe than last time she was here. The rocks have taken over. They have conquered. It is the Land of Rocks.

"You probably want privacy," says Jasper, handing her the cell phone. "I'll wait downstairs."

Flor dials Lita's number. It rings and rings till the message comes on. Of course she won't pick up, Flor realizes too late. Lita won't recognize the number, and she only answers people she knows.

"It's me!" she squeaks after the beep. "It's Flor. I—"

"Flor!"

Her name! Her name pronounced the proper way. For a split second, Flor thinks Mama picked up, but no, it's one of the aunts, she's can't tell which, they all sound alike. She sinks into a chair and a rock jabs her butt.

"Hi, Titi. Is Mama there?"

"No, *mija*. Not right now. How are you all doing? Are you all right?"

Flor can tell she's picturing them in their island hut, chomping on bones, wild dogs roaming the streets. The aunts love the city, bustling in and out of each other's houses, babysitting each other's kids so often the baby cousins hardly know which one's their real mother.

"We're okay. We're just fine." Wait! This isn't what she planned to say. She's supposed to be making Mama come home!

"You're eating? That papa of yours knows nada about food."

"He's taking good care of us." Flor can't help it— she can't let Titi badmouth Dad or the island. She has to defend them. Yanking the rock out from under her, she tosses it on the floor. "And just so you know, precious baby Thomas is fine. Don't bother to ask."

"*¡Mija!* Are you being fresh with me?"

192

She sounds so much like Mama. Tears spurt into Flor's eyes. Who knew it could feel this good to be scolded?

"It's hard, I know," says Titi Whoever. "Flor. Florita! All of us are praying."

After they hang up, Flor goes slowly back down the stairs to the lobby. Jasper and Charles Darwin sit in an armchair printed with fat, cheery robins.

"What did she say?" Jasper asks.

"What?"

"You called your mother, didn't you?"

Suddenly Flor can't trust her voice. She nods.

"I would too." Jasper's face softens. "If I thought I could get her to come back, I'd call my mother every single day."

Jasper never lies. She's just speaking the truth. But somehow she's struck on the very thing that cracks Flor open. Flor presses her eyes with the heels of her hands, which make a terrible dam. The tears spill over. Flor hates to cry in front of other people, because they always try to make her stop. They always tell her *There there, it'll be okay,* and pat her and hand her tissues for her runny nose. Even Sylvie

193

was like that. Especially Sylvie, with her crazy-tender heart. Sylvie would make Flor feel bad about crying, because it got her so upset.

But Jasper just sits there, hugging Charles Darwin. It's not that her green eyes look unkind, or like she doesn't care, but she seems to understand some things you just have to cry over, cry and cry till your insides are scoured out.

"Charles Darwin's mother died when he was eight," Jasper says after a while.

That's so sad Flor cries a little more, but then she's done. Then she sits in another armchair, this one upholstered with bright red cardinals, while Jasper tells Charles Darwin stories. When he was little, he loved beetles. He used to collect them, and once, when he had a beetle in either hand and found a third one, he picked it up and put it in his mouth. It spurted beetle juice! There really is such a thing.

It's a good story. Flor asks Jasper to please tell her another one.

chapter nineteen

That night Flor stays up late, struggling to write her report. She flips through the worn book, read by armies of kids before her. Let it be recorded that not everybody adored Anne Shirley. In the margin beside the part where Anne gives a dreamy speech about how heavenly September is, someone wrote PUT A SOCK IN IT. (Anne *does* talk a lot.) Near the end, where Gilbert, who's always been just a friend, gazes into Anne's eyes, and her heart flutters and a veil or something falls away and oh, perhaps, perhaps—KILL ME NOW, it says in black ink.

Flor pages ahead to one of her favorite parts, where Anne says that what she wants most of all is to add beauty to life. She loves this world so much, and she wants her students to feel the same way. To be happy and curious, and to take joy in all the boundless, bottomless richness of life.

Wait. What is this? Beside that part it says, in a strangely familiar handwriting, HERMOSA. Beautiful.

Flor's pen smears. Her fingers cramp. Confused, she lays her cheek on her paper, just for a tiny second.

Something hits her window. For a groggy moment she thinks it's Joe, throwing rocks, mistaking her for a frozen fossil clock. But when she looks out, she sees something flapping big wings. Very big wings. Stumbling down the stairs, Flor unlocks the front door. Cecilia flies in, bringing with her the cold, hard smells of water and night. Her look is meant to kill.

"Who locked the door?"

"You snuck out?"

"Ssh!"

Flor follows her into her room, where Cecilia shuts the door behind them. Her bedcovers are bunched into a Cecilia-sized shape. Flor gapes as her sister sits down on her fake self.

"It says something on your cheek," Cecilia says. "It says something backward." Her black hair is in a tangle, and a scratch glows on her cheek. Like someone who's hacked her way home through a wilderness, that's how she looks. Cecilia flops onto her back. Smells of earth and dark cling to her. Her eyes close, and she lies as still as a marble statue atop a grave. Oh, no. No! Here they come again, those bony, icy fingers at the base of Flor's neck. That putrid breath on her cheek. Flor grabs her sister's ankles and squeezes as hard as she can.

"Stop!" Cecilia sits up. "Are you trying to amputate my feet?"

"Where did you go?" Flor flings herself down on the bed. "You have to tell me."

"You're not going to snitch on me?" Cecilia looks at her.

"Don't insult me!"

"Promise."

"I'm sick of promises! I detest promises! Okay, I promise." Flor draws a breath. "Cele, this isn't how you are."

Cecilia is quiet for a long while, like she's trying to decide if what Flor just said is true or not. Flor breathes in the room's complicated smell of nail polish, soap, and pencils sharp as weapons. Above them, the butt crack is lost in shadow. Flor runs out of patience.

"You wouldn't do this if Mama was here. You *like* her being gone."

"That ink seeped into your brain. You've got brain poisoning."

"You're a traitor. You're taking advantage of Dad."

"He deserves it."

"You're on her side!"

"It doesn't matter whose side we're on, Flor! Don't you get that?" Cele looks thin around the edges, like a dwindling bar of soap. "How about tomorrow, I'll give you a manicure. And a pedicure. You can choose any polish you want."

"No bribing! I already promised not to tell."

And she won't. She'll lie or steal or do whatever Cecilia wants, to keep her from leaving too. Flor can't spare another person. She tries to touch her sister, but Cecilia picks up her brush and drags it through her tangled hair.

"Oh my God, I'm so tired." She looks it. Not just tired tired, but tired of keeping up her complicated secret life. She pulls the brush through Flor's hair, a quick, Mama-like stroke that makes Flor catch her breath.

Oh, no. The dream. She had it again last night! She forgot, but now it comes back to her. Up on the ledge, unable to see—but last night was even scarier. The dark was gritty, like smoke or saltwater, and she had to hold her breath, because if she breathed it in, something bad would happen.

Something very bad.

Cecilia keeps on brushing Flor's hair, gently now. Flor listens, holding her breath.

"In poems and stories, when a lowly caterpillar turns into a beautiful butterfly, it's this wonderful transformation. But what if the butterfly wishes it could go back to being a nice, plain caterpillar? What if it doesn't want to fly? Maybe it liked living on the safe ground better. But too late. You can't go back in the cocoon once you wrecked it getting out."

Flor's still holding her breath. Cecilia's voice is so

199

quiet, it's like Flor's eavesdropping. Eavesdropping on a demented person. What is Cecilia talking about?

"It doesn't matter how scared or sad you are, it's over."

Not breathing is hard. Harder and harder. Your lungs on fire, your head about to explode.

"Your old life's over," says Cecilia. "You've got to fly."

Flor's jaw unhinges. She gasps. Spittle kablooeys.

"Oh my God." Cecilia pulls the covers over her head. "You need to go away now. You need to go away this second."

Flor staggers out into the hallway. Her ignorant father and innocent brother are sound asleep. Her sister's like a sleepwalker, wandering in the dangerous dark, talking crazy nonsense. Flor's the only one in this house who's wide-awake. Who senses the danger they're in. She knows things she doesn't want to and doesn't know things she needs to. She is the keeper of knowing and unknowing, and how did that ever happen?

"Your old life's over," Cele said. But that can't be. Your life is always your life, now and forever. Cecilia's

200

still her sister. Nothing can ever change that.

In her room she takes out the fossil Sylvie found and the one from Dr. Fife. Fossils used to be for wishing, but wishing hasn't done any good. Yet the fossils still feel powerful. These two were here long before humans, and they're still here, stubborn as she is. They're trying to give Flor a message. Give her courage.

She pushes up her window so the lake, the cruel and powerful lake, can be her witness. Carefully she sets the two fossils side by side on the sill.

"Sylvie left," she whispers. "Mama left. But not Cele. As long as I live and breathe, not her."

chapter twenty

Rain again. Mrs. Defoe gives Flor a C minus on her book report and writes SEE ME AFTER SCHOOL in red.

At indoor recess, Mary Long corners Flor and describes how she was up all night coughing and wheezing. Her mother played cards over at Betty Magruder's house and must've brought home some of Flossie's cat dander. Mary is allergic to everything in the universe, and if there is another universe, she's allergic to everything there too. She's just getting warmed up, describing what happens if she eats raspberries, when Jocelyn grabs Flor's hand.

"Come with me!" She drags Flor across the gym, past the ladies in embarrassing workout clothes doing embarrassing Jazzercise—the school gym is also the island rec center—and over into the equipment closet, where Joe is unpacking boxes of new jump ropes. Jocelyn gets busy hooking a neon-pink one through the belt loop of his jeans.

"Guess what," he says. "My father's going to ask the village council about the clock."

"Really? That's good! That's so good."

"He's sure they'll say no." Joe's shoulders begin to rise, but a look from Flor freezes him midshrug. "At least he said he'd try. That's something, right?"

"If only he had somebody to stand up for him," says Flor. "You know, vouch for him. Besides you, I mean."

"Defoe would be the one," says Joe. "Considering she's in charge of the school and even grown men are scared of her. But forget that. That's never happening."

"Giddyup, Powder-Pink Cloud!" Jocelyn shakes the jump-rope reins. "Fly me up to the sparkle sky!"

Joe gallops around the equipment closet. He tosses his head and paws the floor with his high-tops. Jocelyn's in heaven. Sparkle-sky heaven. Joe's long, thick curls glint in the overhead light, toss like a dark mane. The most surprising boy on the island. The hypothesis is supported.

Mrs. Defoe's personal dictionary does not include the word *sympathy*. After school, she tells Flor she knows things are difficult at home. She's sorry about that. That lasts half a second, and then she's laying into Flor, saying her report was unworthy of her. Did Flor actually read the book? Does Flor know the difference between three hundred and six hundred words? Why is this section smeared? If there's one thing Mrs. Defoe won't abide, it's a promising student wasting her talents. She won't abide it any day, and twice on Sunday!

On and on she drones, saying things she must have said to so many students so many times how can she even stand it, and all the while Flor watches a trapped bumblebee throw itself against the window. The rain has let up, and the sky has a pearly sheen.

She's dying to get up and let the poor bee out but prefers not getting her head bitten off. Mrs. Defoe raps her desk.

"Maybe you could tell me what you think the book's theme is. Since you failed to include that, among other things, in your report."

Flor sits up straighter. She can do this.

"It's about . . . about how beautiful the world is. Anne's in love with it. All of it! Wildflowers and cows and rain and fairy tales and even cranky, crabby old people. She wants everyone else to be in love with the world too."

Mrs. Defoe's eyes narrow. She rests the arms of her bog-colored blouse on her desk. "Go on."

"And she thinks the best way to do that is be a teacher. Her friends are going to be teachers too, and they warn her she has to be strict and give out punishments. But Anne says no. She won't yell or be mean. She wants to be the kind of teacher who wins her students' hearts."

Flor pauses. The trapped bee thuds against the shut window.

"Continue." Mrs. Defoe's tone is what Anne

Shirley would call perilously ominous.

"Well, it turns out one boy's so bad and disrespectful she *does* punish him, but afterward, she feels like a tragic failure. And so she and Anthony—that's the boy—become friends, and he starts to work harder and discover he's smarter than he thought, and it just goes to prove what Anne believes, that there's good hiding in every person, if you only look for it."

Flor flops back in her chair. Mrs. Defoe taps the book.

"Kindly show me that passage, Flor O'Dell."

Flor takes the book and pages through. But before she can find it, she comes to where someone wrote HERMOSA in the margin. HERMOSA, in that neat, pointy handwriting. For a moment, the world spins. Cecilia never writes in books, Cecilia never breaks the rules, but this one time, even she couldn't resist. She loved this part too much. When she was eleven, her heart, her heart too, sped up at the part where Anne says how big, how beautiful our world is.

When Cecilia was Flor's age, she loved the same book. So did Mrs. Defoe. How can that be? How can people so absolutely different have this in common?

A mystery. A mystery Flor almost feels she could solve—if only Mrs. Defoe wasn't eyeballing her, if only that poor bee wasn't having a nervous breakdown. Flor can't bear it another second. She jumps up and opens the window. The bee zooms out into the fresh, rain-washed air. Sitting back down, she finds the section she was describing and hands it over to Mrs. Defoe.

Mrs. Defoe reads. Behind her glasses, her eyes take on a distant, almost dreamy look. A look so un-Defoe it's embarrassing, but also fascinating. Outside, somebody is raking. The *scritch scratch* is the only sound. Mrs. Defoe strokes the corner of her dried-drool-encrusted mouth. She cocks a penciled-on eyebrow, regards Flor over the top of the book, then gets up and walks to the window.

"I once knew this book nearly by heart." She gazes out at whoever's raking. Mr. Hawkins, probably. "I'll confess something, Flor O'Dell. I haven't reread it in decades. I assumed I knew it through and through. But the remarkable thing about good books is, they stay new. Reread this book when you're my age, and I guarantee you'll see Anne Shirley with different eyes."

Flor is absolutely sure that's impossible, and likewise sure it's no time to argue.

"For years I've remembered Anne as a shining crusader against the dark forces of ignorance. But maybe she was more like a treasure hunter. Each of her students was a treasure chest, full of riches for her to uncover." Mrs. Defoe touches a hand to her throat. "I may also have forgotten how easily she laughed."

Mrs. Defoe opens the book and reads some more. Flor sits still, afraid to move. Is she off the hook? Still in trouble? *Scritch scratch* goes the rake. After several centuries, Mrs. Defoe raises her eyes and looks surprised Flor's still there.

"There's no avoiding the fact that you wrote a truly reprehensible report, Flor O'Dell. However, you do know the book." Which she does not hand back. "You are dismissed."

Flor gathers her things and pulls on her jacket. Slipping out the door, she glances back to see Mrs. Defoe, deep into the book, lift her hand to her mouth. It doesn't cover her smile.

It's Joe raking leaves. He's got a big soggy pile.

"Are you really Flor? Or did she murder you,

and you're Zombie Flor?"

"She's not so bad."

Joe takes her head in his hands and examines it.

"What do you think you're doing?"

"Checking for brainwashing."

He's an efficient raker, and it's a pleasure to watch him, even in this drizzle. If the clock worked, Flor could tell how long she stands there before the behavior of the graveyard lilac gets her attention. She crosses the road.

"Come out," she tells it. "I'll introduce you."

"I can't. My father needs me at the quarry."

"Your father won't mind. He wants you to make friends."

Clank clank. She must be wearing her tool belt.

"Joe's nice," Flor says.

"I already know that. My observations show—"

"Did you ever think that maybe you overdo the observing?"

Clank. A hiking boot pokes out, draws back.

"Watching other people is a protective mechanism I developed early in life. When I went to school, the other kids . . . I hate when people stare at me.

Or make a big point of not staring. Or . . . worse. I learned to be alert."

"Otherwise known as hiding."

The bush grows very quiet.

"Sorry," says Flor. "I'm not trying to be mean."

"You are not a mean person."

"Sometimes. Sometimes I am."

"And sometimes . . . sometimes I'm a coward."

This is Jasper-speak for "sometimes I'm a coward." Because Jasper always says what she means. No matter how hard or unpleasant that may be. Being named after a rock truly suits her.

"Joe won't tease you about your arm. I promise. Come on. Please?"

After a moment, "All right," whispers the bush.

Joe's putting the rake away in the shed. His gaze arrows straight to Jasper's belt.

"Whoa," he says. "Some serious tools."

He quizzes her on what each is for. The two of them are members of the same species. The Species of Tool Worshippers. Rain drips off Flor's nose. Pleasure fountains up inside her. As Jasper explains about the trilobites, Joe absently picks up a rock and chucks it

210

at the clock tower. Jasper looks surprised, but then, as if she thinks this must be some kind of initiation ceremony, she picks up a rock too. Winds up and lets fly. The stone vanishes in the mist, then descends in slow motion to settle neatly into the old bird's nest behind the hour hand. Joe gives a low whistle. He regards Jasper with such admiration, Flor possibly feels jealous.

"My right arm is very strong," Jasper says. "It compensates for my left."

"Something's wrong with it," he says. "Right? I mean, left?"

Jasper darts Flor an anxious look. Flor nods encouragingly. Quick, like she's afraid she'll change her mind, Jasper pushes up her sleeve. Joe takes a look, shrugs. For once Flor loves that shrug.

"My uncle in Kentucky, his arm got chewed off by a combine. He got a really cool mechanical one."

"I might get one someday. The correct term is prosthesis."

Joe picks up another rock. But a voice that makes grown men's blood freeze in their veins shakes the air.

"Joseph Hawkins Junior!" Mrs. Defoe's head juts

211

out the window. Her hand, still holding Anne, shoots out. "What do you think you're doing, young man?"

"Umm. I don't know?"

"Just as I thought. Come inside this instant."

So much for any possibility of Mrs. Defoe morphing into Anne Shirley. So much for change. Still 11:16, taunts the stubborn, triumphant clock. *Na na the boo boo!*

chapter twenty-one

On Sunday they skip Mass. Flor guesses Dad's tired of people asking him questions about Mama, and she hopes God will understand. If God is even still paying any attention to them.

Instead Flor rides into town with Dad, who has paperwork to do. His office is in the town hall, and except for them, it's empty. Flor meanders around, twirling chairs, trying out the single jail cell at the back of the building, where Dad sometimes has to lock up tourists too sloshed for their own good. She swings the door shut and sits on the cot, pretending she's a prisoner. For about fifteen seconds. It's horrible. Like you're choking. Or maybe drowning. She bangs the door open so hard, Dad calls, "Whoa!"

"I'm going to take a little walk," she tells him.

The only thing open is the Cockeyed Gull, serving Sunday brunch. A stiff wind's blowing off the bay, but old Violet Tinkiss huddles on the bench out front, Minnie parked at her feet. They're dressed up for Sunday afternoon in town, with a red ribbon in Violet's hair and a matching one around Minnie's neck. Violet's eating a leaky sandwich that doesn't smell too good and not paying a particle of attention to Perry Pinch, who stands beside her, ready to spit.

"Time to move someplace else," he says, and not, Flor can tell, for the first time. When he sees Flor, embarrassment flicks across his face. He juts his chin. "I know you heard me, Violet."

Violet stares straight ahead. Chews.

The Pinches own the Cockeyed Gull, and sometimes Perry washes dishes here. But he can't really care if Violet sits out front. He's just being despicable.

"She's not hurting anything," says Flor.

Perry pushes at his bright hair. It flops right back in his eyes. "She's sitting here cussing out every one of our customers."

"People don't mind," says Flor. "They know she's not cussing them. She's just . . . just cussing. Violet won't hurt a flea."

"If people around here would use their eyes," he says, "they'd see an old lady sitting out in the cold, eating rotten food. Anyplace beside Moonpenny, she'd be in some kind of institution. She'd be way better off."

Violet's gray head wobbles on its turkey-wattle neck. Minnie growls low in her throat. Flor pats the little dog.

"Don't talk like she's not here," she says. "Besides, Violet's always outside in winter."

"Like that means it's right? What made me think you were smarter than that, Flor?"

Queenie and her family, on their way into the restaurant, stop to see what's going on. People coming out pause too. "Looking for more trouble," someone mutters. Betty Magruder stares at Flor in a meaningful way. What? Like she has any connection to him?

"Time's up, Violet!" He says it louder, and now Minnie's up on her two good feet. That dog barks like she's ten times her size.

"It's okay, Minnie," Flor tells her. "Calm down."

"You leave them be, hon." Queenie shoos her hands at Perry like he's a big pesky seagull. "Leave well enough alone."

Minnie barks, people laugh, a baby cries—it's turning into a circus. This'll be gossip for days. Perry's face goes slack. Not a friend in the crowd. They're all on ornery, cussing Violet's side. Perry sets his jaw, but Flor sees it tremble. Just a little, maybe not enough for anyone else to notice. Since Sylvie left, who's he got to talk to? Who's there to understand him? He pushes at his silly hair, and it falls right back in his eyes. Flor tells herself it's his own fault and he deserves it, but right then Perry doesn't look like a bully. He looks like the most alone person she ever saw. Even more alone than her.

Splat! Like a leaky missile, Violet's sandwich flies through the air. Perry stares in disbelief as a greasy string of something slides down his chest and lands on his shoe.

"Bull's-eye!" somebody cries. Minnie hobbles over to lick his shoe. Perry's face darkens. That does it. He grabs the dog's collar and yanks her sideways. Violet screams, leaps up, and pounds him with her bony fists. Minnie howls. Perry staggers back, Flor springs forward, and somehow his big hand closes on her arm. Hard. He's so strong. So much stronger than her. Suddenly Flor is the little girl he used to swing up onto his wide shoulders and piggyback so high, she was a queen on a throne. A star in the sky.

Only she was never afraid of him then.

Quick as he grabbed her, Perry lets go. But his hand left a mark on her skin. His hand let her know her bones are twigs he could snap in two.

All at once, people step back. Dad's here, standing in their midst. He makes everyone feel caught out. A little ashamed of themselves. Minnie stops barking and lies down. Violet sinks back on her bench, as if now she knows she's safe.

Dad pulls a bandanna from his pocket and offers it to Perry. Who doesn't take it.

"Helping out your dad, were you?" Dad asks. "Protecting the family business?"

"Whatever." The word pushes out through Perry's clenched teeth.

"The best thing about living here is, like it or not, we gotta depend on each other." Dad's voice is calm, though his face is worked up. "A place this small, we either have each other's backs or we're sunk. The rest of the world could take a lesson from Moonpenny." He looks around. "By the way, thanks for the good meals you all have been bringing me and the kids. We appreciate your kindness and generosity. I've said it before and I'll say it again—why would a person in their right mind live anyplace else?" He pats his belly. "Only problem is my waistline. Lay off the desserts, will you?"

Everybody laughs, relieved. Nobody's mad, nobody's embarrassed or ashamed—let bygones be bygones. Dad's smoothed everything over, once again. Flor watches Perry slink off and climb into his pickup.

Dad and Flor help Violet and Minnie into the back of Dad's car. He always drives with both hands on the wheel, at ten o'clock and two o'clock. He turns up the east Shore Road, passes the big sign CAUTION:

LOW-FLYING PLANES. They hit a pothole, and Flor's soft brain rattles in her hard skull.

"You let him off the hook," she says.

"Could be," Dad says.

The landing strip is empty, but a swirl of gulls rises on an updraft. Violet and Minnie are asleep, and a sweet, doggy smell fills the car.

"People wanted you to call him out."

"One thing a police officer learns quick." Dad keeps his eyes on the road. "What people want isn't necessarily what's best for them."

He turns onto the rutted road to Violet's house. The neck keeps narrowing, like in a horror movie where the walls of a room press closer and closer. The trees hunch in the wind. Dad hums, no tune she can recognize.

How fast Perry got angry. How big his fists were. How much damage he could do. She looks down at her arm where he grabbed her. How could she have felt sorry for him for a single second?

Violet lives in a fishing shack up on cinder blocks, with a crooked chimney and thorny brambles all around. Dad helps her out, and Flor sets Minnie on the ground. The matching red ribbons flutter in the wind. Think how dark it must get out here. The sound of the lake your only company. Talk about alone. Maybe Perry's right—Violet would be better off someplace else. But she would never go. This place is mapped on her heart with indelible ink.

Now she bows like a wind-up toy, and Minnie follows her inside. The door shuts. A lock clicks.

Back in the car, Dad squeezes Flor's hand.

"I saw you protect Minnie. That made me proud, Flor."

"Thanks, Dad."

Flor doesn't expect another word. Her father's not one to explain himself, let alone defend himself. But wait. The day's surprises aren't over yet.

"Don't get me wrong," he says. "I was tempted to ream that boy out. There's a special spot in hell for those who pick on the weak! But in the end, embarrassing Perry in front of people he's got to live with day in and day out would've just made him angrier. That's the last thing that kid needs."

Every now and then, the thick trees allow a glimpse of lake sparkle. She closes her eyes for a second and sees Perry's jaw tremble. Sympathy pushes at the walls of her heart.

"His life's not so easy as people think," Dad says.

"What do you mean?"

"Never mind."

Dad is too forgiving, Mama's voice says. He'll do anything to keep the peace. Perry will only get worse if he keeps getting away with everything. Someday that boy is bound to really hurt someone.

Flor looks down at her arm. The marks have faded, yet how strong he was, how angry—that's tattooed there.

Dad's not done.

"Everybody wants to feel like their life matters, I guess." It's so un-Dad to talk this way. Flor turns to look at him. His cop cap. His big hands firm on the wheel. "We're all after something in this world. Perry. Violet. You. Your sister." His Adam's apple bobs. He works his lips. "Mama." A long pause. "The heck of it is, Flor? No two people see eye to eye on what happy is."

Cecilia said, "It doesn't matter whose side we're on," and Flor hopes that's true. Because she's got both her parents inside her. She sees through both their eyes. Never, ever will she be able to choose between them.

The trees give way and there's the lake, stretching out forever. The restless water slaps against the silent rocks.

chapter twenty-two

Tonight in her dream, instead of being way up high, Flor's only a few feet off the ground. It's not ground, though—it's water, all around. I can swim, Dream Flor thinks, except where is the shore? Somehow she knows the water is deep. In fact, it has no bottom. In her dream, she finally understands how this can be. It makes perfect sense that something can become nothing. Solid can give way to empty. Alive can become dead.

Flor sits straight up in bed. Her heart bangs inside her. In the mirror, her face is white as an egg.

Usually Cecilia gets a ride to school with Dad, and Flor and Thomas take their bikes. Today Flor says she wants a ride too. It's too cold, she says. You'd think this would raise eyebrows, since Flor has been known to bike in snowstorms, but Dad just says fine, and Cecilia just says she better be ready on time.

The fact that Flor has resolved not to let her sister out of her sight does not occur to either of them.

At school, Joe motions her over.

"You're not going to believe it. It's uncanny."

Uncanny. *Uncanny?*

He glances around the playground, like strange forces are on the loose. They could get ambushed at any moment.

"When Defoe called me inside on Friday? She was nice to me."

"*¡Dios mío!*"

"She asked why I keep throwing rocks at the clock. And then, instead of biting my head off, she actually waited for me to answer. I was so surprised, I told her. And guess what. Uh-oh. Speak of the devil."

Mrs. Defoe steps outside. Her brown jacket is

buttoned to her chin, but what is this? Around her neck is a yellow scarf. Not brownish yellow, but the pure yellow of buttercups. Knotted under her chin, the scarf reflects upward, just the way the flowers do.

Joe and Flor gape at each other.

"Uncanny," whispers Flor. "Is that what uncanny is?"

"We had a conversation. I mean, an actual two-way deal. It turns out she hates the clock being broken too. She said this place should be a beacon of knowledge, but it's giving out inaccurate information. She said getting used to something can be the worst kind of ignorant behavior." Joe pauses for breath. "She got pretty worked up. It was terrifying, like her body was host to an alien force."

They turn to stare at their teacher.

"She said I was right; she bet my father could fix it. She said she knew he had it in him, and it's never too late."

Flor watches Mrs. Defoe finger her bright scarf. Is it possible? Can their teacher be evolving?

"She said some more stuff," Joe goes on. "About how every day is a new day . . ."

"With no mistakes in it yet," finishes Flor.

Joe's eyes widen. "How'd you know?"

"It's from a book we both love."

"*What?* You and her?"

Flor shrugs.

Joe laughs.

The very second school is over, Flor races out the door. She's waiting when Cecilia comes out, dragging her feet in their high-heel boots.

"Let's walk home together," Flor says. "We haven't done that all year!"

"All right," says her big sister.

"Why not? We can— Wait. Did you say all right?"

Cecilia rolls her eyes. She pulls out her lip gloss and coats her beautiful lips.

"Unless you want to go home with your friend."

She points the lip-gloss tube. Jasper stands beside the lilac bush. Not *in* it. Beside it. She waves. Joe, his brothers, and his sister stream by, and Joe stops to do fist bumps. Which Jasper has no idea how to do, so he teaches her.

"I can't go with her." To her own surprise, Flor's

226

disappointed. "I have to watch Thomas." And *you*, she does not say.

"I'll watch him," says Cecilia.

"You will?"

"What else have I got to do?" she snaps. "Name one thing!"

It'll be a long afternoon trying to stick to her. And if she's watching Thomas, she can't go anywhere. She can't do anything stupid or dangerous with him at her high heels.

So Flor and Jasper walk to the Red Robin Inn, which is more or less deserted. All the birders are gone by now. The two of them prowl around, peeking in the different rooms, trying out the beds, looking through a pair of binoculars someone left behind. Jasper makes them cocoa in the microwave. Dr. Fife's still out in the field, though not for long. The sun sets earlier and earlier, shrinking the afternoons.

They take their cocoa out on the porch and sit in the rockers. Jasper's got a new book, photos from the Galápagos Islands, where Darwin made some of his most important discoveries.

"See these giant tortoises? They can live to be two

227

hundred years old. Darwin rode on one's back and clocked its speed at approximately—"

Flor interrupts, pointing to a photo of a bird that resembles a Moonpenny Island cormorant, only with wings so small they're like feathered flaps. It is, Jasper the Endless Explainer explains, the flightless cormorant, a species endemic to the Galápagos, meaning it exists nowhere else. Its ancestors could fly, but once they arrived on their island, they had no predators. They no longer needed to make quick getaways, so little by little, over generations, their wings shrank.

"Wait. Wait a minute. They gave up flying?"

"Umm-hmm."

"I'm sorry, but that's completely birdbrained. Who'd give up being able to fly?"

"The flightless cormorant, that's who. It's perfectly adapted to its environment."

"But . . ."

"People think that evolution is all about getting stronger and bigger and faster. But no. Species evolve according to what they need. Not everyone needs to be big and powerful."

Flor speeds up her rocking chair, like that will

make her brain work better.

"You can ask my father. Some of his favorite trilobites evolved to be blind."

Flor stops rocking so abruptly she almost dislocates her head. "Now you're trying to trick me," she says.

"Why would I do that?"

Flor stares at the empty road. Flossie Magruder trots out of the woods to sit in the middle of it and bite her fleas, serious work that commands every ounce of her attention.

"You wouldn't," says Flor. "So you better explain."

"It's simple. The ocean was getting crowded. There were more and more creatures who could swim fast, which meant increasing competition for food. Also, many more predators."

Jasper pauses significantly. Predators. She and Flor are united in antipredatorism.

"Meanwhile, the bottom of the ocean floor had plenty of food. It had plenty of soft mud to burrow in and rocks to hide under. So some trilobites returned there. It was so dark that little by little, their eyes narrowed to slits, and then . . ."

"Eek!" Flor covers her own eyes to protect them. "I don't want to hear it! It's like a horror movie!"

"Not really. Their going back was better for everybody. Everybody got what they needed."

To live forever in the dark? Who could possibly need that? Parting her fingers, Flor watches Flossie flop over in the road and roll on her back, paws tucked up, her yellow eyes nothing but slits. Slits of bliss.

Jasper is still talking. Her mother and her team have made a big discovery. They found a new species of toxodon, with bigger teeth and a heavier snout. The toxodontidae world is going wild. They may even name the species after her.

Flor tries to be polite. How cool, she says, but inside she's angry. Jasper's mother chose an extinct, big-snouted creature over her! And now she's famous! Is this fair? Is this justice? Meanwhile, sweet Dr. Fife is stuck with trilobites who evolved backward.

As if on cue, he putters around the bend in his golf cart. Flossie gives him the skunk eye, and he carefully tootles around her. He swings into the driveway, just missing the porch, and clambers out.

He's had another glorious day, little animalcules! His eyes twinkle. His socks droop. His white beard has grown so long, he could definitely pass for Santa, if he gained a hundred pounds. When he goes inside, he leaves a little shimmer of joy behind him on the porch.

"Your father's the happiest adult I ever met."

"I know. It gets on my nerves sometimes."

"Really? I wouldn't mind some happy parents, myself."

They rock in their chairs. The day's light is dwindling fast.

"He loves what he does," Jasper says. "Every day, he loves it. He's not in it for the fame. Darwin didn't do it alone, you know. You rarely hear about the other scientists who contributed to his theories, but he couldn't have done it without them. What Father finds out on Moonpenny could help unlock new secrets about the origins of species. That's enough for him, I guess." Her deep laugh. "The trilobite's his hero! Try and get more humble than that."

Flor thinks of her own father. Him and his unmappable ways of the heart. Out in the road,

231

Flossie Magruder quits scratching. Her ears go on high alert. Two seconds later, Perry Pinch's pickup zooms around the curve. Going way too fast. Way too fast! Middle of the road. Spitting gravel. Flossie freezes. Flor and Jasper leap from their rockers.

"Flossie!" they scream as one. "Look out!"

The old cat levitates, all four paws in the air. A blood-chilling yowl, a streak of fur hurtling into the ditch at the side of the road. A dust cloud where the truck was.

"Did he hit her?" Flor whispers.

They stare at the ditch. Be alive, be alive! One beat. Two. Three. Cautiously, a pair of mangy triangles rises over the edge. With a cry from the underworld, that cat vanishes among the trees. Yes! High fives! Flor and Jasper collapse into their rockers, panting with relief.

"He could've killed her!"

"Killed her and not even know!"

"Not even care!"

"He's the most reckless boy I've ever observed."

Anger shoves relief out of the way. Flor jumps back up and punches the air around.

"I wish a predator would devour him! I wish he'd go extinct! I wish—"

"Who was with him?"

Flor freezes midpunch.

"Nobody. Who'd be brainless enough to ride with Perry Pinch?"

Jasper stares. Her mouth goes small as a nickel. "Right next to him." Her voice is hushed, as if Flor's the one who nearly became roadkill. "You didn't see?"

Flor saw. Of course she did! She throws herself down in the rocker, flings her hands over her eyes, only it's no use. Maybe some creatures can choose to go blind, but not Flor.

"It was your sister, wasn't it? Is she in love with him?"

They were arguing. The heat in their faces, the pent-up anger in their bodies. Arguing, just like Mama and Dad.

Flor leaps back up. Thomas! Cecilia is supposed to be watching him! Did she leave him on his own? Has she gone that brainless? Flor runs down the steps.

"Flor, wait! I'll get Father to drive you."

Within moments he's outside, shrugging on his

jacket, revving up the cart, following her directions without a single question. When they jolt to a stop at Flor's, she jumps out. Waving over her shoulder, she sees them looking back with twin faces of concern. If she had time, she'd run back and hug them both.

"Call if you need us!"

"Thomas?" She bangs open the front door. "Thomas? Where are you?"

No reply.

He's not a hiding kind of boy. Call his name, and he's there. Flor's brain, rattling around from Dr. Fife's driving, grows still. She walks from room to room, just in case, looking under beds and behind closet doors. In Cecilia's room she takes the time to knock everything off the desk.

Where? Moonpenny is suddenly big. Enormous. Flor has her bike out, ready to start searching, when she gets another idea. Back inside, she dials Cecilia's cell. Amazingly, her sister answers. Flor can't speak.

"Flor? Dad?" Cecilia's anxious. "Hello?"

"Where are you?" Flor manages to croak. "What do you think you're doing?"

"I'm at the library."

"No, you're not! You liar! You left him! He's gone! He could be drowned, he could be stuffing things up his nose and suffocating. He—"

"Thomas, you mean? He's right here. I took him to after-school arts and crafts."

"What?"

A pause.

"Hi, Flor," says Thomas. "I made you a thing."

"Now do you believe me, you insane person?" says Cecilia, and hangs up.

Your brother almost ran over Flossie Magruder.

Flor hits SEND fast, before she can change her mind.

Then waits. Sylvie has to answer. She can't ignore feline-icide, not tenderhearted Sylvie, who rescues worms from puddles and weeps over squished squirrels.

Cecilia and Thomas come home, and Thomas gives Flor a mess of glued-together Popsicle sticks. Cecilia's eyes are red and puffy. She feels sick. She has a headache and a stomachache, and from the chilly look she throws Flor, you'd think it was all Flor's fault.

So she didn't leave him alone. But she left him, all right. There's no trusting her, not at all. Her sister is a complete stranger. Who knows what she'll do next?

Flor keeps checking the computer. But the rest of the night goes by and . . . nothing.

Just before Dad says to turn it off for the night, Flor checks one last time. And there it is. In purple font.

"I have to tell you a secret."

chapter twenty-three

The next afternoon, Cecilia comes straight home, goes to her room, and locks the door. When Flor puts her ear to it, she hears brokenhearted music. She hears crying. Not really. She *feels* crying, right through the sturdy door Dad hung to give Cecilia her privacy.

Flor leans against the wall. She has the phone. She's guarding it, knowing Sylvie will call. All day she's tried to think what the secret could be, and she can't. Because transparent as just-washed glass— that's how the two of them are.

The phone rings!

But it's Jasper, who's never called Flor before. Over the phone, her voice sounds even deeper than in person. She's calling to say they have set their departure date. One week from today.

"The forecast is for the weather to turn much colder. Father says work conditions will be too difficult."

Flor pictures their attic room. That wild sea of rocks and maps, filmy dust and dirty dishes, specimens in every stage of discovery. Dr. Fife at his worktable, *tap tap tap*ping with his little troll hammer. Jasper in her crazy-big clothes, the president of the Charles Darwin Fan Club.

You'd think you'd get used to having people leave you. Instead, it only gets harder and harder. Flor slides down the wall and sits on the floor.

"Flor?"

"I . . . I have to hang up. I'm expecting a really important phone call."

This is so rude. Beyond rude. What is wrong with her mouth?

"Oh," says Jasper. "All right."

A predator, that's what Flor feels like, big and bad. Suddenly she's boiling over with anger. It's like she gets mad at herself on behalf of Jasper, which makes zero sense.

"Jasper, by every rule of friendship, you have the right to be furious at me!"

A pause.

"I guess I never learned those rules," says Jasper.

"You need to! You definitely need to learn them!"

"All right! Okay!"

They hang up. Did they just have a fight? Decide to be friends? How can things get so complicated with a person who only ever speaks the truth?

The phone rings again.

"I'm sorry," she begins.

"Flor!"

"Mama. Oh, Mama."

"Titi Aurora told me you called."

Flor goes into her room and shuts the door. She wants Mama all to herself.

Tonight, no shouting aunts or laughing cousins in the background. No music or TV. Just Mama, her voice clear and familiar as if she's standing in her spot beside the sink, her paring knife flashing like she's slicing up light itself.

Mama asks about school, and Flor tells her that today Mrs. Defoe wore a pink blouse. Mama laughs. She wants to know how it's going without Sylvie, and Flor tells her terrible. Then she says she met a girl who's in love with Charles Darwin, who was in love with islands and spurting beetles and birds who can't fly. She explains that species evolve depending on what they need, so some of Darwin's finches had fat beaks, but on other islands they had long beaks. Mama says that's interesting, tell her more. Flor tells her it's not about becoming the biggest or smartest. Dr. Fife says every creature is important. Everyone needs something and everyone has something to give. Just like Dad says about the island.

Mama says, "Oh, Flor." And goes quiet for a while.

It's the longest they've talked since Mama left, and it's all about Flor. Not Cecilia, not Thomas, just her. It's nice. It's so nice. It's as nice as when Mama was here, almost.

At last Mama says she's had time to think. To really think.

"I'll be home this weekend," she says.

For good? The words scald Flor's tongue. They explode in her mouth. But she's too chickenhearted to let them out.

"Good," she whispers.

Mama doesn't ask to talk to anyone else. It's like Flor was enough. After they say good-bye, Flor pulls on her jacket and, phone in hand, goes outside. The stars are pinwheels. It's like the quarry, only spread across the sky, light blazing, shining out from so far away, so long ago, from stars that may no longer exist. Things that are here but aren't.

The phone comes alive in her hand.

"Sylvie!" This time it's really her. "I'm sorry! My mother called and . . ."

"It's okay. Only I can't talk long."

Flor's nervous legs want to pace, but a few feet from the house, the connection dies.

"I'm wearing my wild horses T-shirt," Sylvie says.

"Me too!"

"My aunt actually threw it away, but I rescued it."

"We need to get new ones."

"Flor." Sylvie's voice breaks. "Is Flossie okay?"

"She's fine. She's probably got nine hundred lives left. At least."

"That's good."

"I know."

"I never told you what happened," Sylvie says. "Why I came here."

But she did tell. This can't be the secret.

"Your parents think our school isn't good enough, that's why."

"I only told you part, Flor."

The connection dies, and Flor scuttles back toward the house in time to hear Sylvie say, ". . . the rest. You know what Daddy says now? He wants me to be an engineer! Actually, he says I *will be* an engineer! Even though I still hate math. Hate it! I decided I'm going to be a sculptor."

"Really? Sylvie, that's so cool! Why didn't I think of that? It's perfect for you!"

"When I told Daddy, he said I'm too young to know what I want. He said I'll grow out of it. Flor, I'm growing *into* it. Why can't he see that?"

Anger is Flor, not Sylvie. But her voice shakes with it, eleven-plus years' worth of it. It's like anger is the secret she's kept inside, the way the blue-and-green Earth hides her fiery core.

"Now I know why he and Perry fight so much. I used to wish Perry would just do what Daddy said, but now I know. He can't. Oh, Flor, how'd it get to be such a big mess?"

"What are you talking about, Syl?"

"My family. It's been messed up for a long time, and this summer . . . Perry kept getting in more and more trouble, and then he said he was going to quit school, and my father said no way, and they were yelling at each other all the time, and my mother started getting drunk even in the daytime."

"What?" Flor misheard. "What did you just—"

"That's why I never wanted you to come over."

Flor looks up. The pointy stars spear a passing cloud.

"They call it her bad habit, like she bites her nails or watches too much TV. It's the same as saying somebody *passed* because you can't stand to say the truth. They *died*."

The stars shred the cloud.

"It kept getting worse, Flor. She'd turn into this

horrible crying mess. Or else she'd just sit and stare at the wall like a zombie."

How could Flor not have known this? She can't believe her best friend carried around a secret this terrible.

"My father blamed Perry. He said it's because Perry is such a big disappointment to Mom. And Perry said my father's a bully and a dictator and no wonder my mother's so lonely. I don't know which one of them's right, Flor! It doesn't even matter. Because she just keeps drinking."

Mrs. Pinch, always perfect, always beautiful. Flor was so used to seeing Sylvie's mother that way, she never saw . . .

"One night Perry and Dad started fighting for real. Pushing and shoving each other. Grabbing and shoving each other, getting madder and madder. I tried to get them to stop, I begged them and begged them, but they wouldn't."

"Didn't your mother do anything?"

"She was passed out by then."

Mrs. Pinch, so perfect. Mr. Pinch, so powerful he owns the Earth's guts. Even for the Pinches, it had to be hard to keep a secret like this. "That boy's life is harder than people think," Dad said. Did Dad know? Is that why . . . ?

"They both have such bad tempers, Flor. It was the most . . . I couldn't stand it. I had to stop them. And we were upstairs, and you know the stairs, you know how they're slippery . . ."

The stairs in the Pinches' house are made of marble. Special marble Mr. Pinch ordered from a quarry in Italy.

"And my father told me to get out of the way, but Perry shoved him, and I don't know, one of them . . . maybe both of them . . . They didn't mean it! But somehow I fell down the stairs."

"No! No no no."

"They were both so sorry." The anger drains from her voice. "They got me ice, and gave me Tylenol, and they kept saying they were sorry sorry sorry. Perry about died." Her voice hushes, like this might be her fault. "He'd never hurt me on purpose. Never."

"Only he did!" Flor cries. "On purpose or not! And you forgive him, right? You love him no matter what."

"Of course I do! He's my brother! What's wrong with you, Flor?"

"With me? Nothing." But jealousy twists deep inside her. Cecilia loves him too. Loves him and not her.

"Then Perry cracked up the car, and we all flew over to the mainland, and when we got back, my mother—" Sylvie breaks off. Someone, her aunt probably, is talking in the background, and Sylvie answers politely yet with a firmness Flor doesn't recognize. Flor hears a door close.

"Anyway," Sylvie goes on, "the next thing I knew, my father said I was going away to school. He said it would be better for me."

"Sylvie." Flor's voice is louder than she means it to be. "How come you never told me?"

"I don't know! I got so used to covering up about my mother. Every time I started to tell you, something stopped me. Like, I needed to protect her. Or . . ." Her voice catches. "So when my father made me promise not to tell about falling, I—"

"You should've anyway! You should've told me, Sylvie."

"Maybe . . ."

Flor jumps up. She kicks a rock. "I told you all my bad stuff!"

"Flor." Sylvie's voice tenses. "I'm telling you now."

"All that time you pretended everything was okay." Flor kicks another rock. Kicks thin air. Startles some lurking night creature, who races into the field. "How could you do that to me? That's as bad as lying!"

A pause.

"I can't believe you," Sylvie says quietly. "Do you know how hard it was?"

"That's exactly why you should've told me!"

"I couldn't. I just couldn't. And you know what? This isn't about you."

Sylvie's words sting. But Flor knows who's right.

"You know I'm right! How could you just smile and act like everything was fine? You betrayed me. You—"

"Like you're the main one who got hurt? That's so Flor. That's so selfish and bossy and hateful!"

"That's better than being a soggy wimp like you!"

"In case you didn't notice, I'm not anymore!"

Click. Sylvie hangs up. She's gone. Flor stares at the phone. How can this be? She's lost her best, her perfect friend twice.

Flor feels like she's falling. Losing her balance, pitching forward into dark air—it's her dream, but now it's Sylvie's too. Falling, tumbling, reaching for a bottom that isn't there.

chapter twenty-four

Friday morning, the island's in the grip of a wind so fierce, the seagulls hang motionless in the air. Rain sweeps across the back field, wave after wave, like an army marching in formation. Dad drives them to school, then speeds off to check if the road to the neck is flooding. Inside, the big radiators clank away, and the air steams with the smell of wet socks. Fog wraps their classroom in a silver cocoon.

At the end of the day, Cecilia waits for her and Thomas. Flor could faint.

"It's dangerous out," Cecilia says. "Lots of wires

and trees are down. Thomas, hold my hand."

Across the road, the wind yanked an oak out of the ground like a rotten tooth. It's a shock to see how shallow the roots are on such a massive tree. Branches lie all over the place, and chain saws whine near and far. The temperature must have dropped twenty degrees.

This is the island that summer people never see. The steely sky, the dark lake flexing its muscles. The air spits at you. Nothing is gentle, nothing is kind.

Queenie pulls up and says hop in quick. Two Sisters is usually closed Friday afternoon, but she's on her way to open. People are going to want kerosene and candles, not to mention a place to swap information about the storm.

They pass a tree resting against a roof like it fainted. A lawn chair somersaults across a front yard, and the campground sign is upside down. Cottage wind chimes clatter and clang. At their house, a cracked branch of the lilac sweeps back and forth like a witch's broom. Queenie looks worried. Stay inside, she tells them. Don't move till their father gets home.

"Mama's coming," Thomas says. Queenie looks

surprised, then sad.

"The way that fog's rolling in, hon, I wouldn't count on them making the evening run."

The electricity is out. Cecilia switches on the emergency lantern, and they all pull on extra sweaters. Dad calls Cecilia on her cell to say he's got his hands full helping people, will they be okay if he doesn't come home for a while yet? This makes Cecilia so indignant, Flor could faint for the second time in an hour.

"I'm here, Dad. I'll take care of them!" Old Cecilia is back. She's taking charge. "I know, Queenie told us. . . . No candles," she says. "Got it, Dad."

She strikes a long wooden match and gets the oven going for heat, then peers into the cupboards, tapping her lip, frowning her familiar prim frown. Soon she's flipping pancakes, every one perfectly round, no lumps, and so much for being a vegetarian, because she eats four strips of bacon. Applesauce, warmed up, with cinnamon on top. Thomas finishes his milk and for once doesn't use his shoulder for a napkin. From the look of him, he's as grateful as Flor to have his big big sister back. The house is getting

251

cold, but warmth steals through Flor. Her shoulders, which feel like they've been hunched around her ears forever, relax.

Cecilia runs a hot bath for Thomas. When he gets out, she tells Flor to take one too.

"It'll raise your body temperature," she says. Just think—this kind of bossiness used to make Flor angry! "And you can use my body wash if you want."

Cecilia's acting like she loves them. It's uncanny.

Flor lies in the tub. How quiet this world is, the world where nothing mechanical hums or ticks. If only the power would never come back on. She wants to live here, in this moment lifted free of the rest of time. Climbing out of the tub, she feels toasty, smells delicious. They're drinking cocoa when Cecilia's cell rings again.

"Hey. Yes? All . . . hey!" She yanks it from her ear, puffs a breath. "Dead!" And now she can't recharge it. She gives the phone a mournful look. It was You Know Who. Don't think you can fool Flor.

But Cecilia promised Dad she'd stay. Maybe Flor shouldn't believe her, but she does. When Dad comes home, he'll get the emergency generator going and take over, but till then, the three of them are stranded on a desert island and no one can leave. It's crazy how happy this makes Flor. Even Mama not coming tonight is okay, with Cecilia here.

Even though she's regarding them with those dark stranger eyes. Even though she's starting to look stricken with regret. Even though her face is growing so sad, you'd almost think she was gazing on her brother and sister for the last time. Before she tells them good-bye. Before she runs away.

Flor jumps up, spilling her cocoa. She grabs her sister's hands.

"Let's go upstairs! We should go upstairs right now."

chapter twenty-five

Candlelight spins a yellow web in Thomas's room. They've lit every candle they could find, including Cecilia's aromatherapy lavender and the holy ones Lita gives them every Christmas, with pictures of the Sacred Heart and the Merciful Virgin of Guadalupe. Officially Thomas is in bed, but the top half of him hangs over the side. The old lilac bush *tap tap tap*s the side of the house, trying to deliver a message. To remind them of something.

"Remember Town?" says Flor.

Her little brother crashes out of bed onto the floor.

"Can we play can we play please please pretty please with a cherry on top?" He's on his knees, begging like Petey. He remembers Town? He was barely human the last time they played.

"Get back in bed this instant," says Cecilia.

"Can I be the fireman?"

"I'll be the doctor," says Flor.

Cecilia sighs. She half smiles. "You know who the mayor is."

Their town has so many problems. Snowball needs an ear transplant, a tricky operation. Fire breaks out in the bathtub, and Thomas has to rush to extinguish it. When a bad guy tries to steal Cecilia's purse, Officer Thomas has to catch him, and Judge Flor sends him straight to jail. Hungry, the workers order takeout Oreos and milk, special delivered. All the while, Mayor Cecilia sits at her desk, issuing laws and writing proclamations.

"All citizens of this town must be abed by eight thirty p.m.," she abruptly declares. "Which is immediately. By illustrious order of your illustrious mayor."

"Let's vote!" says Thomas. "I vote for fifteen more minutes!"

"Me too," says Flor.

"Two to one!"

"Mayors exercise veto power." Cecilia studies the ceiling, considering. "But since I'm so benevolent, I grant your petition."

Farmer Thomas plants a field of plastic dinosaurs, but what do you know? A noisy construction crew plows straight through it, laying down a new highway. Meanwhile, the mayor puts on her makeup. Blush, lipstick, that smoky eye shadow. Flor watches in the mirror. And then the mayor lifts Flor's chin and brushes color across her cheeks too. She angles her head, considers, wipes it back off.

"Your skin's too nice the way it is," she tells Flor.

"It's sickly! It's the color of a cauliflower!"

"No. It's the color of ivory. You look romantic, like a princess captive in a tower."

"Really?"

"All kinds of boys will fall in love with you, Florita. Take it from the wise mayor of Town."

In the mirror, their heads nearly touch, and for a heartbeat, in the candlelight, it's hard to tell who's who. They merge, they crisscross. *Hermosa,* Flor thinks, and it's like the electric lights suddenly flare on, only inside her. Someday, she will be as old as Cecilia is right now. Future Flor is there in the mirror, waiting, beckoning. This feels so surprising, and the fact that it's surprising is most surprising of all, because of course, of course Flor's always known this. That she will grow up. That she will get older, taller, she hopes smarter, and maybe, possibly, by a miracle, prettier. But up till now, she also knew this: she'd always be the same inside.

Now, with Cecilia's face floating beside hers, she can't be sure. When Thomas gets in trouble, he cries and says he didn't mean it. Can you change into another person without meaning it? What if your own heart becomes a mystery, a map that leads you where you never meant to go? In the mirror Flor can see their breath, hers and Cele's, white moths fluttering around their lips. Little ghost breaths.

And then Cecilia slowly turns away.

"We've got to put this monkey to bed."

Thomas has fallen asleep on the rug, surrounded by dinosaurs and road graders. Cecilia's hands go under his arms, and Flor takes his legs. When did this monkey get so heavy? He swings between them like a lumpy little bridge, and they both start laughing so hard they almost drop him. Cecilia smoothes his hair, tucks the covers up around him.

"Now you," she tells Flor. "Beddy bye."

Shadows lick the walls. A queasy feeling makes Flor sway on her feet.

"I'm not tired."

"You still have to go to bed. I promised Dad." Cecilia picks up her dead cell phone, rubs the screen like she's trying to bring it to life.

"Cecilia! How can you love him?"

"Dad?"

"No! Perry!"

Startled, Cecilia presses the cell phone to her heart. She really thinks Flor didn't know! Thinks Flor is a blind creature crawling in the mud.

"He hurt Sylvie. Do you know that? She fell down the stairs because of him!"

"I know. We don't keep secrets from each other." Cecilia tucks her chin against her shoulder. She won't look at Flor. "He's not perfect. So? Are you? Is anybody?"

258

"You are!" Flor's voice is loud inside her head, like her hands are over her ears. "I mean, you were! Till he messed everything up!"

The lipstick Cecilia put on in the dark is crooked, and her mouth looks too big, like someone else's lips took over hers.

"He didn't mess anything up! You don't know the real story."

"Yes, I do! Don't go with him. He's dangerous!" Desperate, Flor grabs her sister's arm. In a flash Sylvie tumbles down marble stairs, crumples in a heap on the bottom. A car slams into a tree. Cecilia lies in a coffin, a wild rose on her chest.

"Stop it." Cecilia's eyes are bright with tears. "I have to live my life!" She tries to pull away, but Flor's grip is iron.

"Hello? What's going on up there?"

Dad. He's standing in the downstairs hallway. Holding the lantern, he peers up at the two of them. His cheeks are raw with wind, his boots and pants caked with mud.

"Are you all right? Cele, are you crying?"

Her eye makeup is all smeared. Now, now he

chooses to start noticing things!

"I tripped in the dark," she says. "I hurt my arm, but I'm all right."

She's Cecilia—Dad believes her. He's trudging up the stairs.

"What a night! Every time I thought I could head home, something else went wrong. The ferry landing took a hit—two pilings washed out. Flossie ran out into the storm; Betty Magruder chased her and got locked out of the house. The road to the neck's under half a foot of water, so I had to check on Violet. To top it off, fog's socking us in. It's a good one, too."

He massages his wind-burned cheek.

"On my way back here, the darnedest thing happened. I lost my bearings." His features look blurred, as if a giant eraser rubbed them. "It was like a bad dream. I should be able to find my way blindfolded."

His boots track mud all the way upstairs. Cecilia asks if he's hungry. But no, Queenie gave him a sandwich.

"You lit candles," he says, sniffing the air, and they don't deny it. Well, he better get outside and start that generator. Back down the stairs he goes, gripping the handrail, doing his old-man imitation. At the bottom, he turns to look back at them.

"Mama won't be able to get here tomorrow either. Not till the crew can fix that ferry landing."

"Did you talk to her?" asks Flor, but Dad just keeps going.

Cecilia heads straight to her room and shuts the door. Flor sits on her own bed, flicking the flashlight around, spotlighting this and that—her shelf of books, the fossil from Sylvie and the one from the Fifes, her backpack on the floor. She makes the light jitter across the ceiling like a star having a nervous breakdown.

Suddenly her digital clock blinks red. Minutes later, Dad comes back upstairs. The big bed creaks, he groans, and his snoring could wake the dead.

The world hums and ticks, snorts and groans. Flor slips her two fossils into her pocket. Waits.

And tonight when Cecilia sneaks out, Flor follows her.

chapter twenty-six

The fog. In her whole life, Flor's never seen it so thick. It prowls the wet grass, fingers the treetops. Dad got lost out here. Dad! If he can get lost, anyone can.

Flor walks her bike. Lucky for her Cecilia's going slow, like she's thinking things over. Like she still might change her mind and turn back. Once she stops, tilting her head that way she does, listening to her own thoughts. Flor holds her breath. If Cele discovers she's being followed, no way Flor can save her. Because Flor will be dead.

Her sister starts walking again. Picking her way along the edge of the road, skirting the sheets of black water.

Waves of fog, now wispy, now thick. The light on a garage glows like a little lost moon. A stone wall is a beached silver whale. At the bend in the road, a long, dark shape puffs out its own personal fog.

Perry's truck. Idling. Waiting.

Jealousy. Fury. Fear. Twisting and twining, they braid themselves tighter and tighter, turning solid, turning into someone whose name is Peregrine Pinch IV.

Huddled behind a tree, Flor can't see him, only her, and can't hear what they say. Standing beside the truck, Cecilia goes up on her toes and sinks back down. She wraps her arms around herself. Maybe she's telling Perry she changed her mind. It's all over between them. Thanks to her little sister, she's come to her senses. Her sister has opened her eyes at last.

Flor's believing this. She's becoming convinced that she better get home quick, before Cele does, when the passenger door flies open. Her foggy sister climbs in. The door slams hard.

The truck pulls away. Slowly. Flor has never seen Perry drive so slowly. This is terrifying behavior for him. She throws her leg over her bike and starts pedaling.

The dark! While she could still see her big sister, Flor was all right, but now, all alone, her old fear beats up inside her, stronger than ever. The sneaky dark, where invisible things grow and multiply. The snatching, menacing, kidnapping dark. The dark at the bottom of the grave. The dark of her nightmare.

Hard as she pedals, the truck pulls farther ahead, but she can still see its taillights, see it take the turn onto Moonpenny Road. The air in her lungs turns to grit. Sweat rolls down her spine, and her knees become sponges. She knows where they're going.

Her foot slips on the pedal. What are you going to do, Flor? Jump him? He's only three times your size. And those fists. You remember those fists. That hand closing on your arm.

The swim hole, the darkest, most treacherous place of all. Why is he taking her there?

The bones of those lovers, picked clean. Minnows swimming in and out of their skulls.

Something can have no bottom. She knows that now.

Flor leans over her handlebars. Her bike is a speeding train. It's a silver bullet. It's a speeding silver bullet train.

By the time she gets to the quarry, the truck is parked and empty. Flor bends in two to catch her breath. The fog keeps her feet guessing as she goes to the rim, tries to find her way down. Everywhere, mud. Silty, stony mud. Her sneakers are already soaked and her toes curl under, aching with cold. She can make out forms and shapes, but the fog blunts everything.

She might or might not be on a path when she hits a slick patch, and that's it. Her feet fly out from under her, and now she is Flor, the human toboggan. Her bottom bumps over rocks, and her hands snatch at nothing till finally she comes to a stop, lodged between two scratchy junipers. Did she yell out? Maybe. Chest heaving, she stares up at the blank sky, braces for footsteps and angry voices.

But nothing. Nobody comes.

Scrambling to her feet, she rubs her arms and looks around. She's never been down here at night.

Of course she hasn't! The rocks feel alive, fog swirling between them like stony breath, or ancient thoughts suddenly made visible. All the creatures trapped in those rocks for millions and billions of years—what if they really came alive now, like toys after the toy shop closes? They'd recognize her, their fellow islander, and the fossils in her pocket. They'd circle around and protect her.

Flor shakes her head. Crazy! Crazy *loca*! But still. She slides her hand into her pocket to touch her fossils, her bits of this island's secret buried heart. They make her feel less alone. Less afraid of what she can't see.

It's what she will see she's afraid of.

The squish of her sneakers is too loud. Never mind the thump of her blood in her ears.

Nothing moves.

Slowly, she makes her way toward the swim hole. And for the first time, the fog parts enough that she can see clearly. There are the cattails, haunted and trembling. Whispering among themselves.

Something trips her, yanks her to her knees. Flor flings out her arms to break her fall, and a spike rams her open palm. Gasping, she realizes what it is. The grid she and Jasper measured out—she's stumbled into the center of it.

Voices.

"You can't. I'm not letting you."

Perry's anger slams into Flor like a fist. Cecilia says something she can't catch.

"I made up my mind," Perry answers. "There's nothing to say."

Flor wobbles to her feet. Her ankle throbs. As quietly as she can, she parts the cattails, slips between them. Cecilia and Perry stand on the slick, flat rocks beside the swimming hole. Fog swirls on the water's surface. Cold as she is, the sight of that yawning black water makes her colder. Slices through her, picks the flesh off her own bones.

"Please." Cecilia's voice is small. "You've got to listen to me!"

It's true! She's trying to break up with him! Trying to tell him it's all over, and he has to leave her alone. But he won't. Of course he won't! When Cecilia lifts her arm, Perry catches it by the wrist. Her delicate hinge of a wrist. He could snap it without blinking.

"We're done talking." His voice is low and tight.

Flor bites the insides of her cheeks to keep from crying out.

"No more talking," he repeats. "No more arguing. You hear me? We're done with that."

Cecilia starts to cry. She rams her head into his chest, making him lose his footing on the wet stones, and they topple close in a horrible dance. They're much too near the edge now. Doesn't Cele see how close she is to falling into that hungry, greedy water?

Flor goes light-headed. Her dream! Her dream of teetering on a high, treacherous edge. But tonight, Flor's eyes are wide. She's awake. Awake.

"Come on." He's got her elbow. "Let's go. It's late."

"Don't do this to me," begs Cecilia.

Flor's body forgets how to breathe. Forgets how to breathe.

"Let's go, Cele!"

"No!"

"YOU HEARD WHAT SHE SAID! SHE SAID NO! LET GO OF HER!"

The words roar out of Flor, and she's flying forward like a balloon with its air gushing out. Perry and Cecilia fling their arms over their heads. What? Flor's twisted ankle collapses under her, and by the time she understands exactly how slippery the smooth, wet rocks are, it's already too late. Her sneakers scrabble and Cecilia tries to grab her, but nothing can stop Flor's headlong slide. Jet propelled, screaming to wake the dead, she's on her way down. The swimming hole opens its freezing jaws and swallows her whole.

chapter twenty-seven

Cold can hurt like fire, and dark hides a million colors. The black water sucks her down, down, piercing her skin, exploding into nightmare fireworks. Flor kicks her feet and flaps her arms, but every part of her is heavy and bulky and made to sink. The hole has no bottom. The water presses in on all sides

Far away, someone calls her name. The voice wants to catch her—she's a fish and it's trying to reel her in. Flor's so numb, the wall of water is so dense, which way is up? She can't tell. Her lungs beg for air. Her fingers slide across a rocky ledge. The voice calls again, tugging and pulling. Does she really hear it? Or just imagine it?

Flor! Flor!

The water's got other ideas. No way will it let her go, no no no. It's been way too long since it got a victim in its jaws. The cold burns. The darkness blazes.

Flor! The voice won't give up. It's like Thomas, saying the same thing over and over, trying to make it come true. *Flor!* Is it a real voice? Or the voice of a ghost?

Lungs bursting, Flor follows it. Her legs kick back the hungry water, her hands slap it, and now the voice grows louder.

Come on, Flor!

Almost in her ear.

Please, Flor!

Her head breaks the surface, who knew water could be so hard, hard as cement, but she breaks it, and in her struggle to breathe she swallows more water, and goes under again. She's sinking deeper, deeper and deeper yet, but now the tip of her foot glances off something solid. Is it a skeleton, turning to stone, becoming part of the island forever? Or can it be the bottom? A bottom after all? Flor's foot searches for it, finds it again, pushes against it, and it pushes back, she feels it help her, boost her, send her kicking and fighting back toward the surface, where a pale light grows brighter. Her body's so tired, it's like she's pulling two people up, like she's the rescuer and the one getting rescued. Just as she thinks she can't make it, the water gives way, makes way. Arms reach for her and she reaches back, hands grasp her, pull her, and here's her sister's face, only inches from hers. Cecilia's crouching, panting, sobbing, but Flor's swooping upward, light as a silver minnow. Other hands have her, hard fingers dig into her with such force she squawks and struggles. The big hands lower her. Her feet touch ground.

She is saved.

Perry Pinch has her by the shoulders. He lets loose a string of curses, some words Flor has never even heard, then hugs her till her bones flatten. Face against his broad chest, Flor may hear him say "Sylvie." But her ears, not to mention every other part of her, are so waterlogged, how can she be sure?

"Oh my God." Cecilia can't stop saying it as Perry

peels off his jacket and wraps it around Flor. No human ever shivered this hard. Her head may shake off. Someone lined her mouth with tiny castanets. Water streams out her nose and ears and all of a sudden her mouth, a stinking, puking stream that lands on Perry's feet.

"Sorry," she whispers.

"We gotta get you home," he says. "I'll go warm up the truck."

He disappears through the cattails. Cecilia's still crying, shaking her head, saying, Oh, Flor, what were you doing? You are so crazy, you followed us out here, what were you thinking? And then she gives a sob, a sob so big and hard it nearly knocks them both over.

"Flor! I was so scared you'd die!"

"Me too."

That makes Cecilia cry even harder. Flor grabs her sister's ice-cold hand.

"But I didn't. And I won't. I promise, Cele! Not ever! And I won't let you die either."

"Oh my God, you are crazy crazy *loca*. I love you so much."

No one talks as Perry drives them home. The

heater blasts, but still Flor shivers. When he stops in front of the house, Flor takes off his jacket and gives it back. The end. The air is dense with it. In spite of how hard Flor tried, something died after all, and they all feel it. The second Flor and Cecilia get out, Perry speeds away.

Dad doesn't wake up. For once, Flor is glad. Tonight she's sneaking in too. A secret life—she owns one now too. Tiptoe up the stairs, step around three empty milk glasses and a plate of cookie crumbs. Was it really tonight they all played Town?

Not daring to take a shower, she staggers into her room, peels off her wet, muddy jeans, and pulls on sweatpants. Her skin smells like lake. She's all fumbles, her arms and legs so heavy. Cecilia appears in the doorway and stands there like she's waiting for permission to come in, which is, for sure, a first.

"What?" whispers Flor, and her sister sits next to her on the bed.

"Why'd you do that?"

"To save you."

"Save me!" Cecilia looks astonished. "From what?"

How can Cecilia ask? Flor would like to bite her. Sink her teeth into her sister's arm till she tastes hot blood.

"What do you think?" she cries, then lowers her voice to a hiss. "Save you! From him!"

Cecilia leans back on her hands. Laughs a jangly laugh.

Flor jumps up, furious. Furious! What's worse, humiliated. How could she think that saving Cecilia would make her sister love her forever, with a love that never wobbled or changed? That Cecilia would be so grateful she'd never leave? Instead, her sister's laughing in her face.

Maybe *Flor* should run away. Maybe she will! She stomps toward the door, but Cecilia catches the hem of her sleeve. Flor keeps going, and the sleeve stretches and stretches. Her big sister reels her in, for the second time tonight.

"I'm sorry." She pulls Flor down beside her. "Listen. You did save me. But not from him."

"You are in shock," Flor informs her.

Cecilia pulls the comforter off the bed and wraps it around them both. She tells Flor that Perry was

275

breaking up with her. Not the other way around. They're no good for each other. At first they were. At first it was so wonderful, Cecilia felt like she died and came back as someone else, and he said she made him feel the same way, and when he kissed her . . .

Cecilia rests her cheek on Flor's shoulder. She's quiet for a long time.

"The swim hole," she says at last. "That was our special, secret place. Our own world, where we could be those two new people. Not smart goody-goody Cecilia and troublemaker Perry, but just us. We could get away from everything and everybody and just be."

But then the arguments started. Perry was smart, way smarter than people gave him credit for, and Cecilia tried to convince him to take school seriously. He said she sounded like everyone else, and why couldn't she just love him for who he was? The last thing he needed was another person trying to change him. She was the one good at school, not him. So they'd argue and make up and argue and . . .

"People say opposites attract." Cecilia's face is like one of the complicated knots fishermen tie. "And they do. But for Perry and me, it turns out, just for a while."

Mama and Dad. Flor shivers and clutches the comforter. What if that's true for them too?

"Arguing made me so miserable so deep down, I wanted to break up too. But . . . I wasn't brave enough. I hate to make mistakes. It's a bad way to be. You never learn anything, trying to be perfect." Cecilia takes Flor's hand, lifts her fingers one by one. "Perry's way smarter and braver than me. He knew we were only making each other sad. He said he'd already made enough people in his life sad, and he wasn't going to do it anymore."

Flor's heart slides sideways in her chest. She feels it bump against something. Hate—the hate she's cherished for Perry Pinch IV. Flor feels her heart bump against it, feels the hate break into tiny bits. That hurts. Hating someone becomes a habit as sure as loving him does. Letting go of a feeling, even a terrible one—it's hard. It hurts.

"I guess I got it all wrong," she whispers.

But Cecilia pulls the comforter closer around them, and her breath warms Flor's cheek. As if the hating was keeping her cold, Flor begins to feel warmer all through.

"Me too," Cele says. "I got it wrong too. Really,

Flor? You didn't save me from him. You saved me from me."

The scent of wild roses, the smell of new pencils, the smell of Cecilia—Flor breathes it in. If she saved her sister from anything, anything at all, she is glad.

"Something else." Cecilia's voice teeters. "I didn't want to break up because . . . because I don't want to feel all alone."

Their heads tilt together.

"Me either," Flor whispers.

"You're not."

"You're not either."

"I know. I found out."

chapter twenty-eight

Flor waits all day long, till late afternoon. The chilly air buzzes with chain saws, and the ground is deep in leaves. Every tree is bare now, the afternoon light waterfalling through the branches. She rides past the damaged ferry landing, where a crew is hard at work, past Two Sisters, where a sign says SORRY—OUT OF MILK AND BREAD, past the Cockeyed Gull, where Violet sits on the bench, Minnie at her feet. Around the island she pedals, past the school, where the fallen branches are neatly bundled and tied and where Joe and his father climb the front steps, carrying toolboxes. Mr. Hawkins's step is sure and steady. When Joe spies her, he points to the clock tower. Gives her a thumbs-up. Flor waves back so wildly she almost rides into a tree.

Cecilia's cell phone is in her backpack. A one-time-only loan. And when Flor figures orchestra practice (what is a bassoon, anyway?) and soccer practice and tutoring and whatever else Sylvie does on Saturdays have to be over by now, when, the truth is, she just can't stand to wait one more second, Flor gets off her bike. The rocks on the shore are still wet, so she doesn't sit down, just stands on top of one, facing the distant, distant mainland, and calls her best friend's number.

The phone barely gets the chance to ring.

"You!"

"You!"

And then perfectly in synch, like they practiced, like two halves of one and the same person, they cry, "Sorry!"

"I should've told you everything before," babbles Sylvie.

"I was so sad!" babbles Flor. "After you left I

thought I would die. I mean, for real."

"I'm sorry!"

"But you're not really, are you? Sorry? Because it's better for you there. It is, isn't it?"

Sylvie doesn't answer.

"I get it, Sylvie. I get it now, and it's okay. You don't have to be sorry. It's good you went. And you're becoming a sculptor. That's so awesome. It wouldn't have happened if you'd stayed here."

"Do you really mean that?"

Flor clutches the phone. Nods. Sylvie hears the nod.

"So you're really not mad."

"Everybody wants something," Flor says. "I mean, you can't map the ways of the heart, but maybe you can. Everybody wants something big and beautiful."

"You're really not mad!" cries Sylvie.

Out of nowhere, Flossie Magruder steals up beside Flor. She flicks her ragged ear, makes a rusty sound that could be a purr or a growl. Back in the day, whenever they got to make a wish, Flor and Sylvie would wish to understand the language of animals. That was once the biggest, best wish they could think of. Flor bends and pets the old cat.

"I'm mad," she says. "But not at you."

"That night I fell down the stairs, something snapped inside me. I could actually feel it. I thought I heard it! Not a real bone, but some part of me I didn't know was in there. And then I felt something else grow in its place, something stronger and tougher. Do you think that's possible, to grow a bone or a muscle you didn't have before?"

"I'll ask Dr. Fife."

Flossie weaves between her legs. Out on the choppy bay, a bobbing, beady-eyed cormorant disappears, *zoop!* Now you see him, now you don't. The day Sylvie announced she was going away to school, they watched one of those big greedy birds, maybe the very same one, watched and waited, counting the seconds till he came back up. That was so long ago! Uncountable seconds ago. Remembering, Flor feels like she's looking back at someone else, two someone elses, not the Flor and Sylvie talking to each other now. She thought she knew everything there was to know about herself and Sylvie, but now she thinks maybe the real trick of seeing, the kind of seeing humans could really use, is the kind that lets you see through someone else's eyes.

"I'm glad you're sticking up for yourself," she tells Sylvie. "You learned that from me, you know."

"You are my best friend." Sylvie's voice trembles. "I will never, ever, even if I live to be a hundred, have a friend half as good as you."

"Me either."

"Not even one sixteenth."

"Not one billionth."

"Trillionth."

"Gazillionth."

Flossie purrs. It is, for sure, a purr. Out on the water, the cormorant—the flightful cormorant—surfaces. His skinny head gleams. Water drips from his long, pointy beak. Rays of sun zap each drop, spark spark sparkle.

chapter twenty-nine

Mama is coming on the next ferry. This is for sure.

What's not is: will she stay?

They all drive to meet her. Along the back shore road and down Moonpenny. The clock tower says 1:09. Flor resets the car's clock by it.

Flor has her fossils in the pocket of her jacket. Since the night they accompanied her to the bottom of the bottomless quarry, she's carried them with her everywhere.

The *Patricia Irene* is a dot on the bay, still more

the idea of a ferry than the real thing.

The day is so bright, it's hard to believe there's such a thing as the dark. Sunshine hits the asphalt, ricochets. Light tap-dances across the water, radiates from the yellow wood of the new pilings. Jasper and Dr. Fife are already there.

"It's the perfect day to travel!" Dr. Fife's blue eyes twinkle. He and Jasper are leaving on the exact ferry bringing Mama back. The ferry goes round and round, never getting anywhere, but what would they do without it? It's another kind of humble hero.

Boxes of specimens, marked FRAGILE THIS SIDE UP, are heaped on the dock. Jasper wears her work boots and an enormous jacket. No hat today. Her carbonated hair fizzes in the sunlight.

Flor knew Jasper would leave. Of course she knew. But the knowing has bobbed on her horizon, a tiny boat never getting bigger. Till now.

"We never got to do so many things. I never even showed you half the island." That this is her own fault makes Flor sad. That Jasper doesn't point it out makes her even sadder.

The sun pours down. Jasper unzips her jacket.

And what is this?

"Hey," says Flor. "That's a pretty shirt."

Jasper looks down, pretending to be surprised. Pretending? Jasper?

"Thank you. I . . . I ordered it online."

"Let's see."

Jasper slips off her jacket. The shirt is the color of new ferns and makes her eyes look like they invented green.

What's most amazing? The shirt fits. Its three-quarter sleeves end right where they're supposed to. Thomas slingshots over to get a look.

"Whoa. It's like when I put your doll's arm in the fire that time, remember, Flor?"

"No fire," says Jasper. "This is how I was born. This is me."

"You could get a wooden arm, like a pirate leg except—"

"That's enough out of you, mister," says Flor.

But Jasper just shrugs. A Joe-like shrug that makes Flor break into her first smile of the day. Jasper smiles back.

"I brought you a going-away present," she says.

And now Flor feels even worse, because Jasper is the one going away, not her, and she didn't think to bring a gift. Maybe Jasper is better at the rules of friendship than Flor thought. Or maybe she just makes up her own rules. She's holding out a familiar book.

"The Galápagos Islands," says Flor. "But you love that book. Are you sure . . ."

"I'm sure."

"Thank you."

Last night Sylvie called. She'd just had a long talk with Perry and sounded so happy. Something's changed in him. He and her father have been talking, actually talking, not arguing. Perry told Sylvie their father listened when he said he didn't want his life all laid out for him—he wanted to discover it himself. He wanted to make something of himself, he did, but he had to do it on his own. Mr. Pinch may help Perry get a job with a friend of his who owns a trucking business. In Columbus. Where there's a river instead of a lake. Where there are highways that connect to millions of other highways.

"He said you're one crazy-brave little dude,"

Sylvie said, "and I said, like *you* discovered that, Perry Pinch?"

Something else. Sylvie's mother is going to a treatment center. It's nearby, so she and her aunt and uncle will get to visit while she's there.

"I'm so glad," Sylvie said. "I miss her so much."

"I know."

"I know you know."

Dr. Fife produces a bag of chocolate kisses and hands them around. Dad says no thanks, moves toward the edge of the dock. Flor's glad. Looking at his face is too hard right now.

"Last night I read about recently discovered species." Jasper unwraps her kiss with her teeth. "One is the world's smallest frog. Five or six can sit on a dime. Another is an earthworm the size of a sausage. Did you know that Darwin devoted the last years of his life to earthworms? Most people considered worms beneath their notice. But Darwin did worm experiments and wrote an entire book on how worms, which are silent, humble, invisible, and everywhere, slowly change the very ground we stand on."

The ferry's getting closer. Flor can make out the

words on its side. Jasper follows Flor's gaze, shuffles her big work boots.

"Sorry," she says quietly. "You're not interested in earthworms at this particular moment, are you?"

"It's okay," says Flor. One hand holds the book and the other's in her pocket, nervously fingering the fossils. A bird-shaped shadow whisks across the ground, and she's back in her dream, teetering. Will she fall or fly? Why does she have to choose? Because time doesn't stop, for better or for worse.

Cecilia's sitting by herself on a bench. Mama will hardly recognize her. Yesterday she went over to Lauren Long's—for real—and came home with a new, shaggy hairstyle. Who knew that gossipy, snarky Lauren could cut hair like a pro? The hidden talents people walk around with! Last night, Flor found the computer open to a site about summer opportunities for high-school students. Internships. Travel abroad. Study at universities. Scholarships available for excellent students.

Now Dr. Fife flings his arms wide. Chocolate kisses fly.

"Moonpenny Island! A microcosm of Earth's

complex and infinite variety! An old scientist could spend his life studying this place and only scratch the surface." Dr. Fife's goofy, adorable laugh rings out. "Literally and metaphorically!"

Thomas picks up spilled kisses and starts unwrapping them with his teeth too.

You can almost make out the few people standing on the deck. Flor tells herself not to look for Mama, who gets seasick and won't be outside, won't won't.

"What my father's trying to say," Jasper says, "is we might come back."

"What?" Flor whirls around.

"If my father can get another grant, we'll return in the spring."

"Jasper! That's so great! That's such good news! Why in the world didn't you tell me before?"

"It's still only thesis, not yet fact. We can't count on it."

"But still! You might!"

Jasper smiles, and before Flor knows what she's doing, she's holding out the fossil Sylvie found.

"Here's your going-away present," she says. "It's a wishing fossil."

"I've never heard of that."

"I'll show you. Touch the edge. Okay, now close your eyes. Good. At the count of three, we both wish. Ready? One Mississippi . . ."

When Flor opens her eyes, Cecilia's gotten up from the bench. Thomas, mouth kissed with chocolate, is a jack in the box. At the end of the dock, Dad's broad shoulders lift. Because there she is. On the top deck, in a red coat Flor has never seen before. Thinner—she looks thinner. Against the dancing light, Flor can't make out her mother's face. Is she leaning forward, trying to make the patient old *Patricia Irene* go faster? Trying to close that dark gap of water between them, to get back home to them for good and all and forever? Or is that just what Flor wants to see?

Jasper slips the fossil into her own pocket. All those gazillions of years it lay buried, and soon it will be crossing the water, riding in a car, boarding an airplane, and winging through the clouds. Part of Flor's going with it, even as she stays here, with the patient rocks, the restless lake, the sister who slips an arm around her, pulling her so close Flor feels their two

291

hearts beat in time. Their mysterious hearts. Their secret, hopeful, unmapped, ever-strong hearts. *Alive, alive,* their hearts say. *You, me, this so-new and so-ancient world.*

The gulls on the pilings lift their wings at the very same moment. How do they do that? They skim over the sparkling water, rise and press the sky. Now the sun's in Flor's eyes, but still she keeps them open. Squints to see.

Acknowledgments

No writer is an island, especially not me. I owe deep thanks to my editor, Donna Bray, for her patience and faith, and to my agent, Sarah Davies, whose support truly is bottomless. I'm so grateful and lucky that Susan Grimm, Mary Norris, and Delia Springstubb read my pages and shared their gentle but spot-on advice. Thanks are also due to the Vermont Studio Center and the Ohio Arts Council.

Of the books and articles I read about my humble heroes, *Trilobite: Eyewitness to Evolution*, by Richard Fortey, is the gold standard. I also loved learning about Charles Darwin as a private person as well as a scientist. Two books that were helpful and delightful are *Charles and Emma: The Darwins' Leap of Faith* by Deborah Heiligman, and *Darwin: A Life in Poems* by his great-great-granddaughter, Ruth Padel.

A sneak peek at
Tricia Springstubb's new novel,

EVERY SINGLE SECOND

SECRET SISTERS
then

They met on the very first day of school.

The night before, Nella laid out her uniform, a plaid jumper and round-collared blouse. She had new pink sneakers with snow-white laces she still didn't know how to tie.

And she had a lunchbox. Her father had given it to her, proving again that he loved her best. The lunchbox was pink, with her name in sparkly letters. For days Nella had carried it everywhere. That night, it stood on the kitchen counter, waiting to go to kindergarten with her.

Back then, Nella only had one little brother. Salvatore. But her mother was pregnant again, and Nella was sure it was a sister. (Little did she guess that in the coming years her mother would bring home nothing but one fat, squally boy after another.) That night, Mom's back hurt too much for her to bend over, so Nella stood up on her bed for her good-night kiss. The plan was to leave Salvatore with Nonni, their crabby great-grandmother who lived around the corner, and for both parents to walk her to St. Amphibalus Elementary school. Even back in those days, having her parents all to herself was a rare event. Put that together with starting school, and no wonder Nella couldn't sleep. No wonder she had strange dreams of her mother moaning and her father pacing, no wonder she thought she was still asleep when she felt his hand on her shoulder, shaking her. Not gently.

"The baby," he said. "The new baby's coming."

Nella rubbed her eyes. Baby? Today wasn't the baby's day. It was hers. Hers hers hers. She jumped out of bed, hoping her mother would tap her forehead and say, *You're right! How could I forget? Get dressed, Bella. I'll fix you a special lunch.*

But her mother stood clutching the edge of the kitchen table, her lips drawn back in a way that stopped the words in Nella's throat.

Then it was all a crazy confused rush, with her father yelling at her to get dressed, and Salvatore wailing, and a wild ride to Nonni's, where Salvatore wailed even louder because he was scared of the old lady, and somehow they were pulling up beside the school and Nella, shoes still untied, was getting out of the car. Alone. Both her parents looked stricken. Maybe they would change their minds.

"You'll be okay, kiddo." Her father pointed toward the grown-ups standing on the playground. "They'll help you. And—"

But then her mother gave a cry, and he hit the gas.

That was when Nella remembered her beautiful new lunchbox. Still standing on the kitchen counter.

The school was behind the church. On the edge of the asphalt playground stood a statue of St. Amphibalus. His hand was raised in blessing, but his eyes were blank. No eyeballs. This was kind of creepy, but who else did she have? She huddled close, setting her hand on his foot.

Please let me have a friend.

"Look," said a voice. Another pink shoe appeared

3

beside hers. The laces were dazzling white and tied in neat double bows. "We're twins."

That wasn't true. Nella had short, curly brown hair, and this girl had long yellow braids. Once Nella had sat behind her in church, and it was all she could do not to reach out and stroke those silky braids. Besides, her own shoelaces were undone and already a little dirty.

"Don't cry," said the girl.

"I'm not!"

"Are you in kindergarten too?"

"My shoes are untied and I don't know how."

The girl ran away, making Nella start to cry for real, but within moments she was back, dragging a tall boy. The two of them could have stepped out of a fairy tale. She would live in a cottage in the woods, with her father the woodcutter, but he would be a prince, the lonesome kind, looking for true love.

His name was Anthony.

"Tie my friend's shoe," the girl commanded, and Prince Anthony bowed.

He had the same pale hair, but thick and curly. Cinderella, that's who Nella was when he crouched at her feet. He tied her laces in double bows to match his sister's, then stood up tall and straight.

"You two stick together," he said.

"Roger that," his sister said.

A big brother. A brother who looked out for you. (Destined for a lifetime of needy-pest brothers, Nella would always remember that moment.)

The girl, whose name was Angela, had gone to day care. She knew about forming a line, zipping your lips, and raising your hand. By lunchtime, Nella was doing everything Angela did. They were twins after all.

As they went into the lunchroom, she noticed Angela didn't have a lunchbox either. That was comforting, until the lunch lady handed Angela a tray of food. Nella held out her hands, hoping for one too, but the woman, whose hair was trapped in a spidery web, ignored her.

"You don't get free?" Angela asked.

"No, I guess." Tears pushed at the back of Nella's eyes. Why couldn't she get free too? She was suddenly so hungry. The room was so loud. The thought of her beautiful lunchbox, home on the counter, made her miss her mother so much, Nella slumped forward, her head in her arms.

"Bella."

Out of nowhere, her father loomed over her. He hadn't

shaved, and his hair stood on end. He looked familiar but strange, nearly a stranger, in this strange place. With a jolt Nella understood: *The world is much bigger than they told me.*

"Great news, kiddo. You have another brother."

Daddy wasn't big on smiles, but he beamed as if he'd delivered the best news ever.

"What a day, huh?" He ruffled her hair. "He's got a set of lungs on him. I swear he's louder than Salvatore."

Angela sat very still, like a girl trying to memorize everything she saw and heard.

"Nonni will pick you up. Keep Sal out of trouble. Wow, kiddo. You've got two little brothers now. You're Super Sister, know that?"

He dropped a kiss on top of her head and was gone. Leaving her there, red-eyed and lunch-less.

"Your mom had a baby," said Angela softly. "I wish my mom would have a baby."

"A stupid brother!" The words burst out fierce and ragged. "I already got one of those. I want a sister!"

Angela blinked. She broke her chocolate chip cookie in half and put it in her mouth. Nella's own mouth watered.

"Don't cry," Angela said.

"I'm not!"

Angela held out the other half of the cookie.

"I don't got a sister either." Angela leaned forward till their foreheads touched. "You and me," she whispered. "We can be secret sisters."

Nella's mouth filled with sweetness.

"Okay," she whispered back.

AN ANNOUNCEMENT
now

Their seventh-grade classroom swam with the smells of lilacs and B.O. Sister Rosa had made a May altar in a corner of the room, with a statue of the Virgin Mary and armloads of perfumed blossoms. That sweet scent would make you dizzy, if not polluted by the reek of boys yet to learn the word *deodorant*. It was just after recess, where the boys hurtled around the asphalt playground bouncing off each other—like nuclear fission, her best friend, Clem, said. The girls clustered near the statue of

8

old, eyeball-less St. Amphibalus.

Except for Angela, who stayed in to help Sister Rosa.

The way Angela sat on her hands now, Nella knew she was trying not to bite her nails. Her blond braids streamed down her back. Once upon a time Nella was jealous of those braids, but now they annoyed her, like so much else about Angela. She had beautiful hair—why didn't she leave it loose, or at least go for a ponytail? You'd think those perfect braids held her together. You'd think if she undid them, she'd come unglued.

Nella wanted to tell Angela about the braids, but was afraid it would sound mean. Even though Nella no longer wanted anything to do with Angela, she didn't want to be mean.

Nella stretched her legs, her mile-long, ostrichlike legs that refused to stay under her desk. They had that kinked-up feeling—what if she was growing again? She was already a freak of nature, towering over everyone in the class, including Sister. Across the room, Clem's spiky head bent over a graphic novel. Casually, nonchalantly, Nella let her glance wander to the Knee of Sam. Which was, as usual, jiggling like crazy. This afternoon that restless knee had a streak of dried dirt shaped precisely like a fish. Nella smiled. Her face grew warmer yet. Raising her eyes, she discovered Sam looking back at her. *Knee stalker.* He grinned.

"My children!" Sister's voice was honey and cream, the voice of a young woman, though who knew how many centuries old she was. She didn't really teach anymore, just filled in here and there around the school. She'd been Nella and Angela's first grade teacher, and prehistoric even then. Nella loved her so much. Over the years, she'd Band-Aided Nella's scraped knees, and dabbed her cheeks with a snow-white hankie when she failed yet another math test. Sister had taught them all to read and to recite their prayers.

Who made you? Sister asked.

God made me, they chorused back.

At St. Amphibalus, every question had its answer. This drove Clem insane. But she wasn't Catholic. She's wasn't anything, which was so hard to imagine. Clem claimed the word *faith* was just an alibi. *Give me proof,* she said. *I'll give you a knuckle sandwich,* Nella told her.

The classroom door swung open. Sister Mary Anne, the principal, strode in.

Abrupt and thunderous silence.

Sister Mary Anne was a modern nun, with steel-gray hair and a no-iron blouse. She spoke in a low voice to Sister

Rosa, who produced another snow-white handkerchief from her endless supply and pressed it to her lips. Her sweet face crumpled. Was she crying? What was going on? The principal straightened her already painfully straight shoulders.

"Boys and girls," she said. "I have an announcement. One I prayed I would never have to make."

She folded her hands as if she might start praying some more. Everyone was staring. "As I'm sure your parents told you, the diocese has been in financial difficulty for some time. Months ago, Bishop Keller ordered a school-use study to determine which buildings were most effective. That study is now complete. This morning, we received word from His Excellency's office that . . ."

Her lips pursed. Sister Rosa twisted her hankie.

". . . word that St. Amphibalus School will close at the end of this school year."

A lilac petal drifted down and settled on the floor. Nella was sure she heard it touch.

"It's not the decision we hoped for." The principal's voice trembled. "Our school has been the cornerstone of this neighborhood for generations. We hoped to educate your children and your children's children. But such is not to be."

The spell broke. The class erupted. Someone burst out crying. Sister Mary Anne held up a silencing hand, and when she spoke again, all wobble was banished from her voice.

"Here is what will happen. Next year you'll attend other schools. But you'll always remember where you're from. You'll always be St. Amphibalus kids! I trust you to carry our traditions of scholarship and faith out into the world and to be shining credits to our beloved school."

Sister Rosa dropped her face into her hands. More girls started crying. Sam pounded his knee with his fist, obliterating the mud-fish. Clem tapped her pointy nose, looking thoughtful rather than upset. But when Nella looked at Angela, she saw a mirror of her own disbelief.

The principal raised her arms, palms up. The signal to stand.

"Boys and girls, this is a very difficult time for us all. We need to remember the verse from Proverbs: 'Trust in the Lord with all your heart, and lean not on your own understanding.' Now let us pray."

Nella barely survived the afternoon. How could this happen? The school always was and always would be. She could pinpoint the exact lunchroom table where she sat the day Dad came to tell her Kevin was born, and the very desk where she suddenly, magically, knew how to read. The corner of the playground where she, but not Angela, joined the Disaster Dolls Club. The spot beside St. A's statue where she stood, mesmerized, the first time she saw Clem.

Clem. Nella had to talk to her. But when at last the day ended, Clem's father, Dr. Patchett, waited in his car across the street.

"Zoinks!" said Clem. "I have sax."

"Say you're sick! You are sick, aren't you?" Nella grabbed her friend's pointy elbow. (Clem was the definition of *pointy*.) "I can't believe it! I love this school!"

"You do?" Clem looked surprised. "All you ever do is complain about the hideous uniforms and the meaningless—"

"I mean deep down, underneath. I've gone here since I was five years old. How am I supposed to start over at some alien school? Clem! We'll be clueless and friendless outcasts."

Clem's surprise morphed into mild amusement. "Are you forgetting I already did that? Like last year?"

"Oh. I guess so." It was true—changing schools was nothing new for Clem. Dr. Patchett tapped the car horn.

"The mother ship awaits." Clem started toward the car. "Call you after sax!"

"Did she say call you after sex?"

Nella wheeled around to find Sam right behind her. She bent her knees in a futile attempt not to tower over him.

"Very funny." She felt an idiotic blush spreading across her cheeks.

"So good-bye, old St. Amphibian." He pulled off his tie. "Where you going next year?"

"How am I supposed to know? We just found out!"

"My parents said this would happen. Enrollment's way down, and it costs too much to maintain a school as old as this."

Nella bit her lip. She hadn't even known about the bishop's study. Her parents never said a word. That was so typical! Her mother was the world's most impractical person and her father . . . well, Nella and he didn't do a lot of communicating anymore.

"I'm going to give Garfield a try." Sam rocked back on his heels. "Considering how far away St. Moloc's is, plus tuition's higher."

"Garfield?"

Nella was shocked. That school had the world's scariest

reputation. It was at the bottom of the hill, in that neighborhood. Everyone said the place had metal detectors but they didn't work, and all the kids carried weapons. The bathrooms had no doors. Detention was in a rat-infested basement.

Garfield kids were mostly black.

Nella didn't know a single black person.

There were maybe three in all of St. Amphibalus. Not counting Mrs. Turner, who cleaned at night.

Not that this had anything to do with anything.

Her bent knees gave a painful creak.

"We've got to bust out of this cocoon sooner or later. Why not sooner?" Sam's voice was confident, but worry flickered in his eyes. His nut-brown eyes, with their fringe of impossibly thick lashes. What he said next made her heart skip. "You should go too. We could stick together."

Before Nella recovered her voice, an eel slithered in between them. Oh no wait. It was Victoria. Her mascara was running. (No makeup allowed at St. Amphibalus, but Victoria got away with things.)

"Oh my God!" She laid her head on Sam's shoulder. Two inches shorter, she was the perfect fit for him. "We're getting split up! Oh. My. God."

Kimmy and the rest of Victoria's flock huddled around crying. Mob psychology—Nella had heard of it. Sam shoulder-hugged Victoria. He'd be sorry later when he found the mascara smears on his shirt.

"You should go to Garfield," Sam told Victoria. "We should all stick together."

Nella straightened her knees and charged across the school yard. Her little brother Kevin chased her, but she shook him off. On the edge of the yard, in the shadow of the statue of St. Amphibalus, stood Angela.

"I can't believe it," she said softly.

Me neither, Nella almost said. *My head's spinning! My heart's breaking! How could they do this to us?*

But she didn't want to be like Angela. Weak, watery Angela.

"It's not like we have a choice," she said.

Her clumsy, ocean-liner feet started running, and didn't stop till she was up the hill and through the tall iron gates of the cemetery. And still she kept on running, though the stitch in her side was killing her. She didn't stop till she got to the statue of Jeptha A. Stone, 1830–1894, where she collapsed in a miserable heap.